THIS IS OUR RAINBOW

16 STORIES OF **HER, HIM, THEM,** AND **US**

Stories by

Eric Bell • Lisa Jenn Bigelow
Ashley Herring Blake • Lisa Bunker
Alex Gino • Justina Ireland
Shing Yin Khor • Katherine Locke
Mariama J. Lockington • Nicole Melleby
Marieke Nijkamp • Claribel A. Ortega
Mark Oshiro • Molly Knox Ostertag
Aida Salazar • A. J. Sass

THIS IS OUR RAINBOW

16 STORIES OF HER, HIM, THEM, AND US

Edited by

Katherine Locke and Nicole Melleby

Alfred A. Knopf
New York

Compilation copyright © 2021 by Katherine Locke and Nicole Melleby
Jacket art copyright © 2021 by Jes & Cin
"The Purr-cle of Life" copyright © 2021 by Alex Gino
"Girl's Best Friend" copyright © 2021 by Lisa Jenn Bigelow
"The Makeover" copyright © 2021 by Shing Yin Khor
"Paper Planes" copyright © 2021 by Claribel A. Ortega
"Petra & Pearl" copyright © 2021 by Lisa Bunker
"I Know the Way" copyright © 2021 by Justina Ireland
"Balancing Acts" copyright © 2021 by A. J. Sass
"Come Out, Come Out Whenever You Are" copyright © 2021 by Eric Bell
"Devoyn's Pod" copyright © 2021 by Mariama J. Lockington
"Guess What's Coming to Dinner" copyright © 2021 by Mark Oshiro
"The Golem and the Mapmaker" copyright © 2021 by Molly Knox Ostertag
"The Wish & the Wind Dragon" copyright © 2021 by Katherine Locke
"Splinter & Ash" copyright © 2021 by Marieke Nijkamp
"Menudo Fan Club" copyright © 2021 by Aida Salazar
"Stacy's Mom" copyright © 2021 by Nicole Melleby
"Sylvie & Jenna" copyright © 2021 by Ashley Herring Blake

All rights reserved. Published in the United States by Alfred A. Knopf, an imprint of Random House Children's Books, a division of Penguin Random House LLC, New York.

Knopf, Borzoi Books, and the colophon are registered trademarks of Penguin Random House LLC.

Visit us on the Web! rhcbooks.com

Educators and librarians, for a variety of teaching tools, visit us at RHTeachersLibrarians.com

Library of Congress Cataloging-in-Publication Data is available upon request.
ISBN 978-0-593-30394-8 (trade) — ISBN 978-0-593-30395-5 (lib. bdg.) — ISBN 978-0-593-30396-2 (ebook)

Interior design by Jen Valero

Printed in the United States of America
October 2021
10 9 8 7 6 5 4 3 2 1

First Edition

Contents

THiS IS OUR RAiNBOW

16 STORIES OF *HER*, *HIM*, *THEM*, AND *US*

The Purr-cle of Life

BY ALEX GINO

"ARE YOU READY?" Dad asked with a bounce in his voice as he put on his jacket.

"Yes and no." My shoes were on and there was nothing I needed to bring with me. I was ready to leave the house, but I had no idea how to be ready for a new cat.

Scout had been mine since I was born. He was originally Mom's, from before she met Dad, but he claimed me the day I came home. The first time Mom and Dad set me in my crib for a nap, they found Scout curled up with me less than ten minutes later. They were worried he might scratch me, so they kept him out of their bedroom after that, but he would slip into my crib when he could, and once I was old enough to have a real bed, in my own room, Scout went to sleep with me every night, nestled at my side, purring as I drifted off.

"Are you excited?" Mom asked, in nearly the same

cadence as Dad, as she put on her own jacket. My relatives say my parents become more like each other the longer they're together. They even have similar haircuts—kind of shaggy, with a soft part in the middle.

"I guess," I said.

Scout had cuddled with me the day Grandma said that using *they* was ungrammatical and that she was going to call me *she* until I could produce a duplicate of myself. If there had been two of me, one of them would have been able to hold the other back. As it was, I told her she was the one who was wrong and got sent to my room for rudeness. Apparently, I'm supposed to be polite when people disrespect me. The worst disrespect Scout ever showed me was sitting with his butt to my face. And if I reminded him by tapping on it, he would readjust himself into a more courteous position.

Scout died last year. He wasn't there for my eleventh birthday. He wasn't there when I failed my science test because I studied the wrong chapter. He wasn't there to play with all summer long. The day Scout died was the worst day of my life, and every time I thought of cuddling him for comfort, I ached more.

Mom and Dad had told me a dozen times that we weren't replacing him, but that's sure what it felt like.

"I have a feeling they'll perk up when we get to the adoption center," Dad said.

I DID NOT PERK UP WHEN WE GOT TO THE
adoption center.

Cartoon faces of cats and dogs covered the SPCA's glass doors. Inside, a woman greeted us and directed us to walk through the dog area to get to the cats.

I hate dogs. People say you're not supposed to hate stuff, but I do. I hate dogs because they scare me. Even the little ones have sharp teeth, and barking makes me want to curl into a ball. I've never heard of a cat biting a person. Nibbles, maybe, but nothing serious. And meows are much cuter than barks. Scout had a whole *meow*-cabulary. He had his "I'm hungry" *mrew,* his "I'm stuck" *mreh,* his "I'm chasing a thing" *mree-eee-eee,* and his "pay attention to me" *me-owww.* Scout didn't like dogs either. We were a good pair.

I barreled down the hall, trying to ignore the barking toenails clicking on tile, and people cooing about floppy ears. Cats might not have floppy ears, but they have elegant tails, not like these beasts, one of whom was thumping his on the ground so hard I could feel it in my heart.

I made it to the double glass doors announcing KITTY CORNER and burst through. The moment I did, a new wave of emotions flooded me. Every single one of those cats needed a home, needed love. And so had my cat. My Scout, my cuddle buddy, my big brother in feline form. The room felt warm and I started to get light-headed. I didn't know whether I was going to cry or pass out.

"You okay?" Dad put his hand on the center of my back. But his touch made everything feel more real. I had had a cat, a wonderful cat, and he was gone, and would never headbutt me again. I needed to go. Immediately.

"No," I said. I ran out of the cat area, past the dog kennels, and back outside.

Sunshine was good. Air was good. Breathing was good. I sat on the curb and stared up at the sky, watching the wispy clouds drift by.

All of those cats needed homes, but none of them were there the day I crashed my bike and twisted my ankle. None of them were there when I had the flu and a headache so bad I couldn't even listen to music. None of them were there the day Great-Grandma Mae passed away. None of them were my cat, my Scout. They were all cute. Adorable, even. But they were all strangers to me, and I was a stranger to them.

Mom came out and took a seat next to me on the curb. "Too much?"

"Yeah." That was all I intended to say, but the moment I opened my mouth, it was followed by a cry, and once I started, the tears fell. Dad came out to see what was up and sat on my other side as I cried. And cried. And cried. Until I was tired of crying and out of tears.

"You want to go home?" asked Dad.

"We can come back when you're ready," said Mom.

"Yes, please," I said, my voice small.

We loaded into the car, the empty cat carrier still in the trunk.

At home, we didn't put out food and water or set up a litter box. We watched a movie without once being distracted by an excitable ball of fluff. And I went to bed without finding out whether the new kitten would want to sleep with me.

FOR WEEKS, THE CAT FOOD STAYED UN-opened in a corner of the kitchen. The cat toys stayed in the junk drawer. The litter box stayed in the closet. Then, one evening, when I had finished my homework and was packing my bag for the next day, Dad handed me a photo, the kind developed on shiny paper, not a printed-out digital picture. In it, a regally poised tawny cat sat at the bottom corner of a bed, their sharp, black-tipped ears and harsh eyes pointed directly at the camera.

"This is Lynx."

"They're beautiful." Lynx was the perfect name for this slightly wild-looking feline.

"He used to live in a pizza shop, where his name was Tony."

"Lynx is a much better name."

"That's what I thought too, so I changed it."

"This was your cat?"

"Yep!" Dad beamed with cat-dad pride. "When your mom and I got together, we had two cats. Scout had been hers, and Lynx had been mine. Lynx was about ten years older than Scout, and he passed away just a few months after we rented our first apartment together."

"Oh, that's sad." The words sounded flatter than I meant them.

"I was devastated when it happened." Dad paused and looked far away until he blinked a few times. "But cats don't live as long as humans. Lynx had been there for me when I didn't have your mom, or Scout, or you. He was an important part of my life, and when I think of him, I think about being a young adult. When I think about Scout, I think about us being a family, and you being little. And now, when we meet whoever's our next furball, we'll be starting a new chapter for our family."

I liked that idea. We were about to enter a new cat era. Dad looked ready to get up, but I had a thought I wanted to share first.

"Can I say something that might be silly?"

"The truest and most important things are sometimes also very silly."

"Like kittens."

"Exactly like kittens."

I had to stare really hard at my shoes to concentrate enough to say what had been circling in my head since our trip. "I think what really made me upset at the adoption place was when I realized that none of those cats were Scout. That no cat would ever be Scout again." I looked up at Dad. It felt even sillier saying it than thinking it had. "Silly, right?"

"And very true. But also, if we adopt a new cat, we'll get to know a very special critter. One who won't do all the things Scout did, but will do new things. Kitten jumping is an unparalleled joy."

Kitten jumping! I was ready. "Can we try again to go to the shelter?"

"I was hoping you'd ask. Let's go this weekend."

EARTH ENTERED A TIME WARP THAT EX-tended each day into a month and the week into a year. Tuesday, I checked the time nearly a thousand times, so I'm pretty sure I'm right. Wednesday, I tried not to check the time at all, but that was even worse, especially since my tablet displays the time, so I couldn't distract myself with it. Thursday, I mostly jumped around, until Dad asked whether *I* was the new kitten. Friday, I set up the litter box and tried out the food and water dishes in a dozen different spots in the kitchen. And through it all, knowing that Scout wasn't coming back didn't make me as sad as before. Or it did, but I was also getting excited for the kitten to come.

Then it was Saturday. I ate breakfast and did my homework while Dad took his morning jog. There was no way I was going to get any homework done once we got back. We loaded into the car for kitten adoption, take two.

I felt a wave of warmth when we pulled into the adoption center parking lot, but I took a few deep breaths, and got out of the car. "Okay. Let's do this thing."

I bore past the dog kennels once more, with the barking and the toenails and the tails whacking against the tile floor, and on into KITTY CORNER, where cats filled a wall of cubbies.

And again I was hit with the overwhelming number of fluffers needing homes. How could I tell which was the right cat? And what if the right cat for me was having a bad day? Or I missed them in the crowd?

I took a few more deep breaths and focused on the rest of the room while Mom and Dad started peeking into the cages. I walked along the far wall, which was filled with posters and pamphlets about feline care. A few other people were there visiting the cats too, including an older man by himself and a woman with two kids. The older man was befriending an older-looking long-hair, poking his fingers through the holes in the cage to scritch their neck. They looked like they would make a good pair, watching TV on the couch together. I was glad someone was there to adopt an older cat, because I wanted the youngest kitten I could find. I wanted my new kitten to remember me from as early in their life as possible.

I approached the wall of cages, focusing more on the info sheets attached to each one than the cats inside. It was easier to say no to pictures than to the cuddle beasts themselves. I found a set of four gray twelve-week-olds nestled into a pile of fur, with names that were all puns based on the word *cat*, like Catapult and Catastrophe.

A stout woman with white hair, wrinkles, and a clipboard approached us. "Hi there, I'm Audrey. Can I set you up in a room to meet any of these critters?"

"What do you think?" Mom asked me.

"How about one of these?" I pointed at the gray cat pile.

"Which one?" asked Audrey.

"Whoever's the friendliest," I said.

"Well, this bunch has been a little shy when we take them out one by one, but let's see how it goes."

Audrey led us through a door marked VISITATION AREA and into a small, windowless room filled with cat toys. There was a chair, but I was glad my parents were the kind of people who knew you had to get down to a cat's level if you were going to learn anything about them. A minute later, there was a brief rap on the door, and Audrey set down a carrier. She still held her clipboard in her other hand.

"This is Catsup." She opened the carrier door. "I'll leave you for a bit."

"Here, kitty. Here, Catsup!" Mom picked up a cat toy and dragged it along the floor. Catsup followed the crinkly pink butterfly with their head but kept their body inside the carrier.

"Let's give them a minute," said Dad.

We sat quietly as Catsup slowly poked out their head. They sniffed around and then cautiously stepped out. Their fur was sleek and gray, almost silver. They smelled my shoe, followed by Dad's and Mom's, then crawled back into the carrier to curl up under the blanket.

"We can take a hint," said Dad, chuckling.

Scout had been shy around strangers too. I had never been a stranger to Scout, but I would always be to this cat. This was not my kitten.

"What do you think?" asked Mom. "Should we go look some more? There were lots of cuties out there."

"I guess," I said. I had guessed wrong once. Maybe I would have better luck next time.

Dad closed the door of Catsup's carrier and we went to find Audrey. There were two more small rooms in the visitation area. One was empty. A couple of adults met with an orange cat in the other. There were also two larger rooms with windows, and cat info sheets attached to the doors. There was a single cat in one room, a ten-year-old named Chonky. He was cute and had an adorable fat belly, but when I waved at him, he turned his butt at me. Not my cat. The other room listed five twelve-week-old kittens, all black, but I could only spot two, both sitting by the window.

"So, how did it go?" asked Audrey.

"Shy guy," said Dad.

"Well, you're welcome to look around, and let me know if there's anyone else you'd like to meet, or if you have any questions."

"Where are the other ones?" I asked.

"The other ones?"

I pointed at the black cat info sheets. "There are five, but I only see two. I know they're black, but that doesn't make them invisible."

"Oh," said Audrey. "Some of these should go." She consulted her clipboard and took down three of the pages. "There are only two left. It's not worth moving them, but once they're adopted out, we'll get a larger litter in here. Do you want to meet them?"

"Yes, please."

Audrey let us in and we settled in a triangle on the floor. The two kittens jumped down from the window immediately and came over to sniff us. One climbed over Dad's knees while the other rubbed my hand with their head. Their fur was so soft I squealed.

"Well, that's a good sign," said Dad.

The kitten that I had been petting went off to sniff Mom's shoes while the one that had climbed the Great Knee Range pounced on the finger I tapped on the floor. Dad picked up a toy and tossed it across the room, and the two shadows flashed after it.

Mom found a long stick with a fur mouse dangling from one end and went fishing for kittens. They skittered, leapt, and pounced. Mom gave the stick to me, and I waved it back and forth, pulling it up occasionally. The kittens reacted to my every move. And when I put down the stick, one of them pressed up against my leg. And if you think that's cute, the other crawled into my lap. Both closed their eyes immediately, and if I didn't move, they would be asleep within a minute. I could hear and even feel their purring.

"Mom? Dad?" I looked as serious as I could manage. "I don't think I want a new cat."

"Oh," said Dad, while Mom matched his surprise with her eyes. "You looked like you were liking these two."

"Exactly. I don't want just one kitten. I want two!" I gave a smile so wide my teeth hurt.

"They make a good point. Choosing would be hard," said Mom.

"And two kittens aren't much more work than one," said Dad.

"Less, even, when you consider they'll keep each other busy."

And that's how Midnight Lightning and Starlight Thunder came to live with us.

THUNDER AND LIGHTNING WEREN'T THERE the time I had to wear an ugly ruffly skirt for Aunt Meg's wedding, but Scout wouldn't be there at the end of eighth grade, when Grandma and I argued over my graduation outfit. Scout might have cuddled me when I had that fight with my best friend in fifth grade, but it would be Thunder who would rest at my side when my crush told me they didn't like me that way. And both Thunder and Lightning would be there the day I had my first kiss.

The way Scout used to tap me with his paw to get me to pet him, Lightning now used the more direct method of pressing his head into my hand. And all three of them liked to climb on top of the fridge and watch me as I made my breakfast.

Just as I remembered a life before Thunder and Lightning, I learned to remember a life after Scout. And someday, a long time from now, maybe when I'm an adult with my own kid, Thunder and Lightning will be old, and someday, they will die too. And then, when we're ready, we'll adopt a new kitten or two, who will be like and different from the ones who came before, and we'll love them too.

But for now, it's all about Thunder, Lightning, me, and a laser pointer. Zoom!

Girl's Best Friend

BY LISA JENN BIGELOW

YOU WOULDN'T GUESS it by looking at her, but Roxy Bellwether was a witch. She could brew a mean anti-pimple potion and fast-forward through ads with a blink of her eyes. In other words, she was pretty good. Yet no one at school had a clue.

Most magic users lived where they could practice freely, in the middle of nowhere or in big cities, where *normal* meant nothing. Not Roxy's family. Her father's passion for medieval manuscripts had plopped them at the edge of a straitlaced college town. People wrote nasty posts on the neighborhood message boards if you painted your mailbox the wrong color. Witchcraft would not go over well.

When Roxy grew up, she could move wherever she wanted. In the meantime, she longed for a friend she could trust with her secret.

Next to the Bellwethers' was a paint-peeled cottage that had sat vacant for months. When a moving truck pulled up in late June, Roxy's mother set her to baking a tuna casserole for the new neighbors. Magic would've made the job faster, but some things were best done the ordinary way, no shortcuts. They walked across the lawn to deliver it.

A girl with twirling, twining dark hair opened the door. Roxy blinked. It was Tess Thomas.

Tess had moved to the ritziest neighborhood in town last fall. The Kingfisher Cove clique had immediately absorbed her, but to Roxy, only Tess's trendy clothes fit the part. Her eyes always seemed to be studying something far away. Sometimes her lips quirked or she said something that made her friends laugh, but her expression quickly misted over again. Tess, Roxy felt sure, was a girl with a secret, too.

And now she stood in the doorway of the ramshackle cottage. Roxy fizzed with curiosity. Curiosity and hope.

"Hi," Tess said.

"Hi," said Roxy.

Their mothers beamed and sent the girls out to play, as if they were six instead of twelve. It was weird. Now that Roxy had Tess to herself, she had no idea what to say besides, *What the almighty heck are you doing here?* And that seemed a bit rude.

"So. Um. Want to see my house?" Roxy asked.

Tess shrugged and followed her.

The Bellwethers' shaggy gray dog bounded up as they entered. He barely glanced at Roxy, heading straight for the newcomer. Tess's face lit up as he barreled into her, tail thumping. "Hello there, handsome! What's your name?"

"Jackalope," Roxy said. "Jacky, for short." She craned her neck toward the kitchen. She hoped nothing incriminating lay in plain sight—no jars of pickled frogs' feet, or neon pink potions simmering on the stove. But there was only the aftermath of the tuna casserole.

Tess rubbed Jacky's ribs. His back paw began to thump.

"Do you have a dog?" Roxy asked, hoping for an in.

Instead, Tess's expression dimmed. Her hand stopped. Jacky whined. "Not anymore," she said.

"Oh. I'm so sorry."

Roxy waited for Tess to continue. Had her dog died, or gotten lost? But Tess only straightened and asked to see Roxy's room.

At dinner, Mrs. Bellwether said, "Tess's mom works full-time, and money's too tight for camp. I told her Tess can come over anytime. I hope that's okay."

"Did she say why they moved here?" Roxy asked.

"It's not really our business," said Mrs. Bellwether.

"Our job is to be good neighbors and friends. Can you do that?"

Roxy didn't stop to think about it. "Yes."

BEING A GOOD FRIEND WAS EASIER SAID

than done, of course. Fortunately, Jackalope was happy to help.

Whenever Tess started to fidget with her phone, Roxy would say, "I know! Let's play fetch with Jacky," or "Let's walk Jacky to the corner store," and Tess would agree. When it was rainy, they watched movies with Jacky curled on the couch between them.

One day, Roxy hooked up the old baby trailer to her bike, and they rode to the lake with Jacky in tow. He rushed in after a family of ducks, barking his head off, then rushed back out when he realized the water was *wet*. He shook himself, drenching the girls.

It was the first time Roxy heard Tess really laugh, a throaty outburst too wild to contain. Their eyes met, alight, and a thrill went through Roxy. This was the moment of connection she'd been waiting for.

Summer glowed brighter after that. Still, a fog always crept in eventually, miles of it separating them. Often it happened when Roxy asked an ordinary question, like where Tess's father was, or whether Tess had any siblings, or whether she kept in touch with her Kingfisher Cove friends. Tess gave short, vague answers (dead; sort of; not really). Each time, she was lost to Roxy the rest of the day.

Probably Roxy should've known better. Who would move from Kingfisher Cove into that crummy cottage if they had the choice? Whatever had happened to Tess's family, it couldn't have been good. Roxy stopped asking questions, her friendship with Tess at a foggy standstill.

Only Jackalope could break through the clouds. Tess made such a fuss each time she saw him that Roxy had a new secret, an embarrassing one: she was jealous of her dog. She wanted more than anything for Tess to smile, for real, at her.

Roxy texted Malcolm, her closest warlock friend, telling him about Tess's mysterious, misty expression. *What should I do?*

Because she could do anything with the right spell. She could make Tess confess her secret. She could make her forget it altogether.

But just because you could do it didn't mean you should. Messing with people's minds was the worst kind of magic.

What's the big deal? Malcolm asked. *She's mundane. How interesting could her secret possibly be?*

Roxy bristled, but he had a point. She and Tess were having fun. Why wasn't that good enough?

But she knew why. Roxy longed for a friend who knew everything about her and accepted her just the same. If Tess trusted Roxy with her secret, then maybe Roxy could trust Tess with hers.

One day after Tess left in her usual haze, Roxy told Jackalope, "I bet she'd tell you what's up."

Jacky cocked his head as if he understood perfectly.

"I know," Roxy said. "I'm being ridiculous."

Then she stopped. She texted Malcolm again. *Help me with something?*

He responded immediately. *Is it about that girl?*

Maybe, she said, unwilling to admit her motives were that obvious.

Her phone rang. Malcolm's face appeared, singing, "Roxy's got a crush!"

"It's not a crush," Roxy retorted.

She'd watched friends moon over other kids, movie stars, teachers. They dreamed about kisses and dates, weddings and babies. This wasn't that.

She simply wanted to spend every spare minute with Tess. She wanted to know what she was thinking, share secrets and opinions, explore every inch of town on their bikes. To snuggle under a blanket, watching a movie, leaning her head on Tess's shoulder, holding her hand while Jackalope snored beside them. To share her magic with her and know she wouldn't freak out or treat her any differently.

She didn't need more. She didn't want more.

She tried to explain, and for once, Malcolm listened quietly. She asked, "Is there a word for what I feel?"

"Yes," Malcolm said. "You have a squish."

"A squish," she echoed.

"Like a crush, but platonic. You're not looking for some ooey-gooey romance. You want to be friends. Good friends."

"Best friends?" Roxy asked.

"Maybe even better than best," Malcolm said.

It wasn't grammatical, but somehow it made perfect sense. "I have a squish on Tess," Roxy said. The words were sweet and tangy, like blackberries, on her tongue.

"Now," Malcolm said, "what are you going to do about it?"

Roxy told him her idea.

THE FOLLOWING WEEK, WHEN MRS. BELL—
wether was shopping, Roxy stood in a clearing in the woods, shivering despite the heat. She held a necklace, a clay disc on a leather thong. Baked into the clay were a dozen magical ingredients Roxy had pinched from her

mother's pantry, plus a tuft of Jackalope's fur, bound by an incantation Malcolm had dug up. Jacky himself she'd left at home. He'd only complicate things.

"Here goes," Roxy whispered. She slipped the necklace over her head.

The trees zoomed up as her body shrank and sprouted ginger fur. Roxy's nostrils flared, catching the scent of squirrel and rabbit, toadstools and ferns. Her ears pricked with birdsong and insect buzz. Her whiskers vibrated.

She wanted to run. Not to anywhere or from anything. Just because.

So she wriggled from the T-shirt and shorts puddled at her paws and ran, ears flopping, tail dancing. She followed a chipmunk's scent to the edge of the woods, where she startled a pheasant. It rose into the air, gobbling. Roxy barked joyfully.

Time to get down to business. Roxy ran for Tess's house and barked at the door. When nothing happened, she stood on her hind legs and swiped at the doorbell. It took several tries, but then footsteps thudded. Tess, in her pajamas, squinted out.

Roxy whined. Tess looked down in surprise. "Oh! Hello, puppy."

Roxy wagged her tail, tongue out.

Tess laughed. "You're cute. Where's your person? Do you have a tag?" Her fingers brushed the leather thong.

Roxy panicked. If Tess removed her charm, she'd be lying on the stoop, human—not to mention naked—with a lot of explaining to do. She ducked out of Tess's reach.

Tess shook her head. "Okay. But someone's going to miss you."

This called for a distraction. Roxy bounced in a circle and barked—the kind of bark Jacky gave when he wanted a walk. Tess had had a dog. She must know what it meant.

Sure enough, she smiled. "Fine. Let me get dressed."

As soon as Tess returned, Roxy darted for the woods. Tess followed. The trees grew thicker with each step. Every few seconds, Roxy circled back so Tess wouldn't be left behind.

She had new sympathy for Jackalope, whose obedience skills were spotty at best. The world held so many distractions for a dog! It took all Roxy's concentration not to investigate each rustle in the undergrowth, roll in a surprisingly fragrant pile of deer poo, and chase a squirrel whose chatter, though incomprehensible, was clearly insulting.

Finally, they came to the creek. The sun through the canopy dappled the water's glassy surface with diamonds. Roxy hopped onto the fallen tree where she loved to sit with a book and a sandwich. She held her breath, waiting for Tess's reaction.

"Oh," Tess said softly.

Roxy exhaled, reassured.

Tess climbed onto the tree and gazed at the water. She seemed to retreat inside herself, leaving a Tess-shaped shell. So Roxy did what any self-respecting dog would do: she nosed Tess's elbow.

Tess came back to herself with a chuckle. "Looking for a thank-you? I owe you one. It's beautiful here." She stroked Roxy's fur. Roxy melted against her.

Though Tess said nothing else, Roxy didn't mind. This, she felt sure, was only the beginning of her new-and-improved friendship with Tess. She slumped beside Tess, laid her chin on her knee, and fell asleep.

She woke in a hurry when, sometime later, Tess stretched and said, "I'd better get back. I'm due at Roxy's for lunch."

Of course! Why hadn't Roxy thought of this? She had to make it back to the house before Tess. She scrambled down and dashed into the woods before realizing Tess might not remember the way. She forced herself to keep to a trot until the trees thinned. Then she tore ahead, ignoring Tess's cry of "Puppy! What the heck?"

In the clearing, she pawed off the necklace. She rose, pale and goose-pimpled, the wood's sounds and smells suddenly muted. She felt dizzy—from the transformation, or the gravity of what she'd done?

There wasn't time to figure it out. She yanked on her clothes, shoved the charm in her pocket, and dashed for the back door. She barely made it before Tess knocked on the front door. Roxy greeted her, panting, Jackalope at her side.

Tess looked at her strangely, and Roxy blushed. "What?"

"There's a leaf in your hair." Tess plucked it out.

"Oh. Um. How did that get there?" Roxy tossed the leaf out the door.

Tess had already turned her attention to Jacky. "Have you seen a dog wandering around?" she asked Roxy as she petted him. "Ginger fur?"

Roxy's heart raced. "No. Why?"

"I saw one this morning. I was going to show you, but it ran off." Tess shrugged. "Hopefully it was headed home. It's no big deal."

No big deal? Roxy wasn't sure whether to be relieved or annoyed.

She texted Malcolm that night. *I DID IT.*

Her phone began to ring. "And?" Malcolm shouted.

"It worked!" She told him everything. "It felt so good. So natural. I could have stayed a dog forever."

Malcolm, who until now had shared her enthusiasm, grew sober. "Careful, or you might."

"What's that supposed to mean?" Roxy said. "The charm worked like, well, a charm. Tess didn't suspect a thing."

"That's just it," Malcolm said. "I've done some more research, and the charm has one serious side effect. If anyone ever catches you, collars you, makes you their pet? You'll stay a dog forever. Promise you won't let that happen."

Roxy had never known Malcolm to be such a worry-wart. "Promise," she said impatiently. "Got any more grave warnings for me?"

Malcolm sighed. "Don't chase cars? Seriously, I hope this girl is worth it."

THE NEXT MORNING, AFTER HER MAGIC lesson, Roxy transformed and lit out for Tess's. Malcolm's warning faded in the light of Tess's joy when she saw the dog on her doorstep. Once Tess was ready, they were off to the creek.

Today, Tess had brought her journal. Roxy tried to read over Tess's elbow, but the writing made no sense to her canine brain. Besides, the trio of turtles sunning themselves on a rock was far more interesting. Roxy flattened herself to the ground and stalked them until *plop, plop, PLOP!* The turtles disappeared into the water. Roxy barked indignantly.

"Stop bothering the locals and get up here," Tess said with a laugh. And Roxy didn't mind one bit, because it meant sharing Tess's PB&J and falling asleep as Tess massaged her neck.

The day after that, Roxy didn't have to ring the bell. Tess was waiting. So the summer passed, and, gradually, Tess began to open up.

First, she said little things. "I miss Coco, but you're sweet, too."

Then bigger things. "I tell Mom I only miss Coco, but I miss Cadence and Nia, too. I hope they're okay."

Another time she said, "Really, I miss everyone but Wally. Sometimes I dream about him. Bad dreams. Like that one time—except in my dream, I'm not there to get help, and Mom—" Her fingers gripped Roxy so hard she yelped.

"I'm sorry!" Tess gasped.

Hot tears seeped into Roxy's fur as Tess's story spilled out. How her mom had met rich, handsome Wally a couple of years ago. How everything seemed like a fairy tale, from the way Wally called Tess's mother his queen to the palace he bought in Kingfisher Cove. But every fairy tale had a villain. When Wally was in a bad mood or had too much to drink, his temper flared, and his fists came out.

"My friends didn't know," Tess said. "How could I tell them? They said I was lucky to have a stepdad like Wally. He fooled them all."

Roxy imagined running across town and biting Wally

where it really hurt. But she'd probably end up in the pound, or worse.

Instead, she licked Tess's hands and face, and Tess whispered, "Things are better now. We're safe. He can threaten and beg and wave his checkbook all he wants. We're not going back."

All afternoon, Roxy sneaked glances at Tess. Now she had an idea where Tess went when she got that sad look. More than ever, she wished she could squeeze Tess's hand. *I know the truth. You don't have to carry your secret alone anymore.*

Of course, she couldn't. Roxy had wanted to gain Tess's trust, and she'd succeeded—sort of. Because while Tess had opened up to Dog Roxy, Human Roxy got the same old clouds. As for telling Tess she was a witch? Forget it. If Tess discovered what Roxy knew and how she knew it, she'd never trust Roxy again, in any guise. Roxy had forgotten the most basic rule of magic: some things were best done the ordinary way. No shortcuts.

There was only one solution. The ginger dog had to vanish as suddenly as it had appeared.

But as Roxy knelt in the clearing that night, a hammer in her fist, she couldn't bring herself to destroy the charm. Her time with Tess had been too precious. Besides, the dog was Tess's only confidante. How could she take that away?

ONE MORNING STRETCHED INTO TWO, THEN
three. Soon, Roxy lost count. Mrs. Bellwether com-
plained that Roxy was falling behind in her magic studies, but Roxy didn't care a smidge.

She and Tess explored new territory, Roxy leading the
way with her curious nose. Tess picked wildflowers and
wove them into crowns for both of them. Roxy mugged
for the selfies, tongue lolling. Roxy stole Tess's cheese
and crackers from her bag. Tess laughed at the crumbs in
Roxy's whiskers, even as she scolded her.

When Roxy stopped to think about what she was
doing, her stomach churned with guilt. It was as bad as
mind magic, really. Tess told the ginger dog things she
wouldn't tell Roxy, even if they were just opinions about
movies or gossip from her Kingfisher Cove friends. But
Roxy couldn't stop.

Sometimes Roxy felt sure Tess knew the truth. It was
the way Tess gazed at her with an expression that could
only be called scrutiny. Not that Roxy could blame her.
Lately she'd had to struggle against the urge to roll in
freshly mown grass. To pounce on garter snakes sun-
bathing in the driveway. To turn around three times before plopping onto the couch. She couldn't help it. These
things just felt *right*.

"Sure you haven't seen a ginger dog lately?" Tess asked.

"Nope," Roxy said, ears flaming.

Then there was the way Tess started calling the dog Foxy, "because of your red coat, and the way you always sneak off before I can show you to anyone." The rhyming name seemed too perfect to be pure coincidence.

In a way, Roxy hoped Tess *had* figured it out, so she could stop lying. But Tess hadn't come out and said anything, nor shown Roxy a single one of the selfies. In a way, she was leading as much of a double life as Roxy was.

One day, as Roxy lazed belly up on the creek bank, Tess spoke tentatively beside her. "I know you're not officially mine, but maybe you could be." She pulled a collar from her bag.

Malcolm's warning felt like forever ago, but it must have sunk in. The buckle's clank was an alarm bell. Roxy leapt to her feet.

"I'm sorry!" Tess cried. "I didn't mean to scare you. But, Foxy, aren't you my friend?"

Her plea pierced Roxy's heart. She didn't flee. Instead, she gazed into Tess's eyes and thought.

Her plan had backfired. She was more tangled in secrets than ever. And she'd grown used to being a dog— loved it, in fact. She could be Tess's secret-keeper, snack sharer, snuggling companion, forever.

It was tempting to stay, to bend her neck for Tess and that pretty collar. But Roxy knew, in her heart, that being Tess's friend was only one dream. Was she willing to give up on all her others? Was she willing to leave her other friends and her family behind?

As Tess reached out again, Roxy growled and sprinted for the clearing. Human now, she got dressed, then slumped at the base of an oak, buried her face in her arms, and sobbed.

Was it because she'd nearly been trapped by her own spell? Because she couldn't give Tess what she wanted? Or because she couldn't have what she, Roxy, wanted so badly: for Tess to see who she really was, and like her—maybe even love her—for it?

Mrs. Bellwether was in the kitchen chopping herbs, whether for a potion or a pot of soup, Roxy didn't know. "What is it?" she asked, seeing Roxy's puffy face.

"I don't feel well." Roxy hiccuped. "Can you tell Tess I'm sick?" She couldn't bear to see Tess, who'd probably be her closed-off, cloudy self again, and pretend everything was all right.

Mrs. Bellwether felt Roxy's forehead. "Go up to bed. I'll check on you in a little while."

Roxy nodded, willing her chin not to crumple.

"And take Jackalope. He always makes me feel better when I'm feeling crummy."

Jacky hopped up from the floor and wagged his tail. Roxy burst into tears all over again.

THE NEXT DAY, ROXY DIDN'T GO INTO THE woods. She hid the charm in her underwear drawer until she'd have a chance to destroy it—because this time, she vowed, she would. She wondered whether she could pretend to be sick until September.

She was practicing cracking eggs into a bowl with a wave of her hand when there was a knock at the door. The levitating egg crashed to the floor with a splat. Jackalope skidded over to lap it up.

"Go get the door," her mother said. "I've got this."

Tess stood outside, wearing a new expression. Wary. Nervous. "Hello," she said.

"Hello," said Roxy, just as wary. It was as if they were meeting for the first time again. "You're early."

Tess shuffled her feet. "Can you come for a walk?"

"It's fine," called Mrs. Bellwether before Roxy could ask. "Go. Take Jacky." For the first time, Roxy wondered whether her mother wasn't as clueless as she seemed.

Reluctantly, Roxy slipped on her shoes as Jackalope danced around. "Where are we going?" she asked.

"Wait and see," said Tess.

Roxy didn't need to wait. She knew immediately.

Her stomach dropped as Tess led her through the woods toward the creek.

Neither spoke until they came to the fallen tree. Tess said, "You know this place, don't you?"

Roxy nodded, eyes on a twig tugged along by the water's current.

"And you know the ginger dog."

Roxy nodded again. Fiery humiliation and icy fear flooded her body. She wished she knew a spell to melt into the ground.

She waited for Tess to accuse her, to demand an apology. Instead, Tess climbed onto the tree and patted the wood beside her.

Roxy couldn't help it. She had the urge to hop up beside Tess, to lean into her, the way she had when she was a dog. But Jackalope beat her to it. Tess's hand smoothed his shaggy coat as the impossibly long moment grew impossibly longer.

You can't tell her. She'll hate you. She'll tell her friends, and their parents will write nasty posts on neighborhood message boards, and pretty soon your family will be run out of town.

Yet there was little question Tess already knew the truth. And she was still here, watching Roxy, not a hint of clouds in her eyes.

Maybe this isn't the end, after all. Not if I tell the truth.

Roxy took a deep breath. "I need to tell you some-thing."

Tess waited.

Roxy clenched her fists, as if she could squeeze the words out. "I was the dog. I . . ." She took another deep breath. "I'm a witch."

She slumped to her knees on the creek bank. The cold water slid through her fingers.

There was a series of soft thumps, and Jackalope's face was in hers, licking her cheeks. Then came a gentle hand on her shoulder as Tess sank beside her. Quietly she said, "Thank you for telling me."

"How did you figure it out?" Roxy asked.

"It was lots of little things," Tess said. "The hardest part was considering the possibility. After that, it didn't seem so ridiculous. If I had to imagine you as a dog, that's how you'd look. Ginger fur to match your hair. Hazel eyes. Cute; floppy ears."

Roxy reached up indignantly to touch her decidedly non-floppy ears. Then she shrugged. Tess had called her *cute*.

"But you never let on," Tess continued. "I thought I must have imagined it all. I bought the collar to see how you'd react."

"It was a test," Roxy said. She felt like a fool.

"Sort of," Tess said. "I mean, I figured the worst thing that could happen was I'd get a pet out of it."

"Actually . . . ," Roxy said, and then she told Tess how close she'd come to choosing the collar and staying a dog forever.

Tess's jaw dropped. "That's horrible!"

"Is it?" Roxy swallowed the bitter taste in her mouth. "You liked that dog. You liked it better than me."

"That's not true," Tess protested, but Roxy held her gaze, and Tess gnawed her lip. "It's just . . . dogs are easy."

Roxy heard all the things Tess wasn't saying. Dogs could be trusted. They didn't judge. They never turned on you.

Roxy stared at her shoes. "I'm sorry. I deceived you and betrayed you. You have every right to hate me."

"I'm too confused to hate you," Tess said. "Why did you do it?"

Stumblingly, Roxy tried to explain. "Think about it," she said. "Would you have ever told me—human me— why you moved here?"

"Of course," Tess began, but then she stopped. "Eventually. Maybe."

"I got impatient," Roxy said. "I really liked you, Tess. I just wanted to be friends."

She waited for Tess to ridicule her. Who'd go to

such extremes to make a friend? *A witch with a squish, that's who.*

But Tess nodded. "I believe you. You've been here for me all summer, when no one else was, even when my head was miles away."

"I'll understand if you don't want to see me anymore," Roxy said.

Tess hesitated. Roxy's stomach sank. Jackalope whined, looking back and forth between the two of them.

Finally, Tess said, "Can you do me one favor?"

Roxy knew Tess would ask if she could sometimes turn into the ginger dog, for old times' sake. And Roxy knew she'd say yes. It was the least she could do, one small way to make amends.

Instead, Tess said, "Can you make me one of those necklaces?"

Roxy almost yelled, *Are you kidding? Of course!* Then she stopped. If word reached the wrong people, the Bellwethers could kiss everything they knew goodbye. They'd have to move to Siberia or something.

As if reading her mind, Tess promised, "Please. I won't tell a soul."

Roxy recognized the look burning in Tess's eyes. She'd seen it in the mirror so many times. It was longing.

She asked, "Haven't you had enough of secrets?"

Tess thought it over. "Some secrets are dangerous,

but others keep you safe. The trick is to know the difference."

"What will you say if people ask what you're up to?" Roxy asked.

"That's easy," Tess said. "That I'm hanging with my best friend."

Roxy blinked, and Tess smiled. For real. At her.

THE REST OF THE SUMMER, FROM BREAK-

fast until dinner, they barely left the woods.

They hunted rabbits and rolled in the mud. They wrestled and played chase, and when they were exhausted, they drank from the creek and curled up in the sun to nap, nestled so close they could feel each other's heartbeat.

In fall, they'd go back to school, and who knew what would happen then? Would they grow closer than ever, or would they drift until they were strangers once more? Sometimes Roxy wished for a crystal ball, but maybe it was better not to know. There were no shortcuts, after all.

Until then, they were two dogs: one ginger, the other black and curly. Three dogs, if Jackalope came, too.

39

40

It's MAKEOVER TIME!!!

It really is pretty fun, actually. I got these leather suspenders out of the last one.

I've never had a makeover before. I'd always thought it was something that only happened on TV. But... I think...I kinda want to, actually.

Hey, Dad. Can me and my friends go to the thrift store after school today and, also, can you drive us?

It'll be super chill, I promise!

44

46

I think my deal is... I dunno, what does this look like to you?

Academic floral.

Knitwear punk.

Cozy ghost.

Oh! That one! Cozy ghost. I want to look like a cozy ghost.

One more thing, fam. You gotta pick your own Porcupines jacket, because you're one of us.

I'll help you put the studs in if you want!

I want a yellow one!!!

Paper Planes

BY CLARIBEL A. ORTEGA

I AM THE only person in my home who can speak with the outside world. Well, maybe that's not totally true. My mami and papi might buy the notebook paper and even tell me what to write, but I'm the one who makes the paper planes. My family can speak to neighbors and friends in Spanish just fine, but there are other people they need my help talking to. Mostly bill collectors, sometimes my teachers, stuff like that. In the faraway place, my family didn't have to worry about not being understood, because everyone was like us. But here, we are surrounded by people who give us looks and whisper about us when they think we can't hear or understand.

I stood at our bedroom window, a thin piece of paper in my hand. I folded it into an airplane, running my fingers along the sides so a small pink light sealed the folds. I placed it beside the twenty other identical paper airplanes on the ledge and opened the window. There was one more letter, in my back pocket for the girl down the street, but that one was a big secret.

Outside, our neighbors went in and out of the bodega with arms filled with cleaning products, or carrying tiny packages I knew were greasy, hot, and delicious sandwiches. My mouth watered as I picked up the first paper plane and sent it flying out the window. It wound around the iron bars of our fire escape, made a few loops in the sky like a bird, and then swooped between two buildings across the street before disappearing. Today, the letters were going mostly to the bill collectors who sent letters in a bright red font to my parents, asking them for payments they didn't have with words they could not read or understand. Some letters were to family at home, in the faraway place. Every letter I sent made me tired, but I couldn't think about that. I just had to get it done because I was the only one who could.

I was rubbing my eyes and about halfway finished when a bright blue truck pulled up to the building across the street. I perked up: it had been a long time since anyone had moved here. I watched closely as someone hopped out of the front seat of the truck. She was tall, with long pink hair and a glittery pink hat. She had *a dog.*

"¿Casi terminas?" My mami stood in the doorway,

her knitting needles working on a new quilt, suspended in the air beside her.

"Yep, almost done," I said, smiling quickly at my mami, then looking back at the woman across the street. Our building was on a narrow one-way street, only wide enough for one car, so I could see across the street pretty well. But I'd never seen anyone so tall or glamorous or beautiful. Except on TV. A soft summer breeze tousled her long hair, and I wondered if it was a wig. The air smelled sticky and sweet and you could almost taste the frío-fríos from the carts on the sidewalk. I wished so badly that I could have one. But my parents wouldn't be able to buy one each for all four of us kids, so it was better not to ask. I didn't want to make them feel bad.

I sent out a few more letters, not paying as much attention as I should have but I could do it with my eyes closed. I couldn't stop staring at the lady. She was directing some movers, waving her large hands and bright pink fingernails as the men carried a furry sofa and leopard-colored lamps up to her apartment. When she walked, her fancy pink boots click-clacked loudly on the sidewalk, an echo swooping through the alleys. What was a rich person like that doing moving to a neighborhood like mine?

"¡Flor, a comer!" my father said. Time for dinner. I had lost track of time staring at our new neighbor. I still had four letters left to send and maybe, finally, one more after that. I thought of Kayla, the girl from school I couldn't stop thinking about. We weren't friends exactly, and at first I thought I just wanted to be her friend or admired her or something. But lately it felt like it was more than that. I just wasn't sure what it was. I sent the last four letters as quickly as I could, and they shot out like a small swarm of bees. Then I took the letter to Kayla out from my back pocket. I stared at it and smiled even though my stomach felt like I was going down the highest drop of the tallest roller coaster. I'd written it months ago, and every day I told myself I would send it, but I was never brave enough to.

"Today is no different," I sighed, and tucked the letter back into my pocket.

A thick stew sat in a pot in the middle of our dinner table. Our mother served us all with a big metal ladle. The stew was salty, and as its aroma reached my nostrils, my curly hair frizzed up and got even curlier. I took big bites of white rice and chicken and wiggled in my seat a bit, my "happy-food dance," Papi called it. All through our noisy family dinner, with my three younger siblings arguing about some video game as they tried to explain the plot to our confused parents, I thought about our new neighbor. The woman with the pink boots. I had never seen someone like her in my whole entire life. I yawned, so tired even my bones felt sleepy. Twenty letters was a lot to send in one day, and I was having a hard time keeping my eyes open.

"You okay?" my mami asked in broken English. I wished she would practice more, but she barely had time to sleep, with two jobs. If she learned and Papi learned, I would get to rest and not have to have bill collectors yell at me. I didn't like how those letters made me feel. They were always in big, bold red letters and I could feel them shouting. It made my stomach ache and my palms get all sweaty, like I was in trouble. The worst part was explaining it again to Mami and Papi, watching them get real quiet and sad and knowing there was nothing I could do to help.

I nodded and smiled, and my mother smiled back, her eyes crinkling. I couldn't help but notice how dark the circles under her eyes were, and it made my heart sink. I wanted her and my papi to be able to be *my* parents, not the other way around, but I knew that right now that couldn't happen. I had to keep being strong for them.

It was hard to sleep that night. Between the sirens and my siblings snoring, everything was so *loud*. But nothing was as loud as my thoughts. I stared at the roof of the bunk bed, my thoughts scrolling across the wood: Kayla and Mami and Papi and the woman with the pink boots and bills and worries and fear. They scrolled over and over like the credits of a television show, but when I placed my finger on the words, they stopped. I traced *Woman with the Pink Boots,* and as I did, the letters turned pink with the spark of my fingers. I startled at a thought: What if?

My heart began to thump against my chest. I'd always felt a little different, because I'm not like the rest of my family. What if she was different too? Maybe she could help me?

She didn't look or act like the other adults I knew. She dressed in bright colors and moved like she was in a play, her arms and hands looping in big, exaggerated movements. When she'd laughed at something one of the movers had said, she had thrown her head back and let out a loud laugh like the church bells on Sunday. She didn't seem serious and quiet and boring like some of the other grown-ups on my block, who judged you for any little thing. She looked the way my heart felt sometimes, too loud and too bright, and maybe that meant she would understand what I was feeling lately. I could write her a letter, not put my name on it or anything, and then maybe she would write back. My letters worked that way. If you wrote a message and sent it, it would find its way back to me. The letter began composing itself from all the words above me, the words of my fears rearranging and disappearing to just one sentence: *Is it okay for girls to like other girls?*

The loud click-clack of boots against the sidewalk woke me. I sat straight up, forgetting like I always did that I was on the bottom bunk, and knocked down all the words above me. The alarm clock on the dresser said 3:00 a.m. in rainbow colors, and the click-clack of boots got closer. I threw the blanket aside, scattering the letters everywhere, and crept to the window, looking behind me to make sure my siblings hadn't also woken up. I peeked over the windowsill and saw her. The woman with the pink boots. She was walking quickly down the street, wiping her eyes with one free hand and holding her cell phone to her ear with the other. She was yelling at someone named Anthony. I couldn't hear exactly what she was saying, but she was telling him off, I knew that much. She stopped in front of her door, facing my building, and yelled one last thing at whoever Anthony was before throwing her phone in her bag. She spun like the ladies in my mother's tele- novelas do and walked into her building. I watched as a light on the fifth floor turned on. I looked behind me again—I wasn't supposed to be snooping and sneaking. I'd gotten in trouble for it before, but I couldn't help it. I was nosy.

The woman went into another room, then came back and closed her curtains, but she didn't close them all the way. I could still see her. I tried not to look, but I wanted to make sure she was okay. She rubbed her temples, then took off her wig. Then her lashes and her dress and a weird bra thingy she had around her chest that gave her boobs. She didn't look like herself. Maybe without these things she didn't feel like herself either. The same way I didn't always like being my mom's niña, my mom's little girl. Sometimes I felt like something else. I took a deep breath and pulled a piece of my special paper from my drawer, and one of my pencils. My eyes darted between my siblings, my note, and the woman across the street. I wrote as quickly as I ever had, then folded the paper carefully into a plane, sealed it, and, before I could think again, sent it out into the night air, praying it wouldn't get stuck on a star. It didn't. A night breeze picked the paper plane up in gentle hands, carrying it up and out of my window. It glided through the air, making graceful loops like a sparrow. Then, finally, the letter floated into the woman's open window, and I held my breath.

Maybe this was a mistake. What if it got me in trouble somehow? She could send the note back and watch it go into my room, because even if I closed the window, the paper plane would keep insisting. The woman was wrapping her real hair up in a scarf when she noticed the letter, and her mouth made a perfect little circle like she was the surprised emoji. I kept looking back at my siblings, rubbing my sweaty hands on my nightgown and biting my lip.

She read the note, and it seemed to take forever, although I know it was only a minute or two. Everything moved in slow motion, and then, finally, she raised one sharp eyebrow and smiled. Then she shut the light off, closed her bedroom window, and pulled the curtains all the way shut this time. Darn.

In the morning, there was a note. Not one to send out . . . a returned note. I rubbed my eyes and quickly jumped out of bed. I walked slowly to the window, so afraid of what the note might say. What if the woman in the pink boots was mad? What if she had caught me snooping last night? What if the note was for my parents? I wouldn't be able to hide it from them; the note would just keep appearing until I read it to them.

Breathe, just take it easy, I told myself.

I grabbed the letter and opened it before I could change my mind. Sweat dripped from my forehead and onto the paper, turning into watercolor flowers, purple, yellow, black, and white.

Beneath my question—*Is it okay for girls to like other girls?*—a word appeared in flourishing cursive.

Yes.

I looked up, but the woman with the pink boots' window was still closed and her curtains drawn.

I kept reading—there was a question beneath her answer.

Are you okay?

I closed my eyes and held the note close to my chest. I thought I was fine, but nobody had asked me that in a long time and now I felt all shaky and sick. Maybe I wasn't okay.

I grabbed a pencil and scribbled my answer quickly.

I don't know. I think I'm confused. And then: *How do I tell a girl I like her without her hating me?*

I sealed the note quickly and sent it. It swooped up, up, way up so high I thought it would fly right into the sun. I looked up as it circled above our buildings and then spiraled back down slow as a feather before landing on the woman's windowsill. It would sit there waiting until her window was open; I couldn't just leave it around my house. My parents wouldn't understand all of it, but I was so scared they might be able to figure parts of it out. Plus, they'd ask me questions about who I was sending notes to. I was scared. My body shivered and I wrapped my arms around myself. I had never, ever said those words out loud, that I liked a girl. Because I knew what that meant, that I wasn't like my parents or brothers. I'd heard my aunts talking to my parents once, when a cousin of mine came out. They'd whispered words like *shameful* and *shocking* and how *God wouldn't like it.* I didn't want my parents to think of me that way.

I spent the rest of the day at the park with my dad, throwing a ball around and thinking about the woman in the pink boots. There were a billion questions I wanted to ask her, but what if I hurt her feelings? Back home, I ran to my room to see if there was a note waiting. Sometimes my brothers hid them from me. They couldn't read them, but it was still annoying, and every day they learned more English. Eventually, they'd be able to figure it out, and then I'd be in big trouble.

My heart pounded and I felt sweaty everywhere as I walked toward the closed window. We weren't allowed to leave windows open when nobody was home, it made it too easy for people to break in. I opened the window and sucked in a sharp breath of surprise when I saw the note sitting there.

My fingers fumbled as I opened it and read the woman in the pink boots' response: *What are you confused about? When you're ready, and it feels right, you tell her how you feel. But only when you're ready. You can't control how she'll feel in return, though.*

I wrote back: *I'm confused about what it means if I like girls. Also, thanks. What's your name?*

My hands shook as I lifted them to send the letter.

Maybe because I knew I was different but I was afraid to be. I let the letter fly into the sky, and this time it flew in jagged starts and stops, almost like it didn't want to go. Almost like it was feeling what I was feeling. It moved like a bird with a clipped wing, but it made it to her ledge all the same.

Why is this so hard? I asked myself. Right then, the window opened. The woman with the pink boots took the note. I watched as she read it and wrote a response, then sent it back in fluttering loops to my window. The sun caught on something on the edges of the paper and it sparkled like a flowing river. When her letters came back, they always moved gracefully. They weren't hesitant or wild like mine were sometimes. She could see me now, because it wasn't dark anymore, and she waved. Her bright blue robe, the same color as the moving truck, was trimmed with tons of feathers. They swayed with the movement of her arm and one came loose. It floated all the way to me, landing softly on my nose where my freckles were and tickling me. I laughed and waved back.

Her note was dusted in shimmer, probably from her makeup: *The answer is in your heart. Sometimes it takes a while to find your truth but you will know when the time is right. Don't rush yourself. My name is Alexis. What's yours?*

For a moment, I wondered if it was okay to tell her

who I was. Before, I had been worried she would tell my parents and get me in trouble. She didn't seem like she would, plus . . . I really needed someone to share my secrets with. So I went to my drawer and grabbed a special pen, a bright blue one I only used for holiday cards and special messages. I turned, looking at my reflection in the mirror next to our window. *You can do this, Flor,* I thought, then I took a deep breath and carefully spelled out my name. I sent the note, and after that we talked back and forth for hours. She told me she used to live in California and that her dog's name was Rufio, and I told her I loved to dance and wished I could fly far away instead of doing my math homework. I even forgot to eat, and one time my mami almost caught me sending a letter when she brought in a plate of tostones with fried cheese. Alexis watched me for a few moments, then sent another paper airplane.

That looks gooooood, she wrote. I stretched the gooey, golden fried cheese and shared with her.

The piece of paper made room for as many notes as you needed to send. It shouldn't fit, but it did, and over the next few days we talked and talked whenever I had the chance.

Who is Anthony? The one you were yelling at? I asked one day.

My ex. I moved to get away from him, but he keeps hounding me, Alexis answered that night.

Are you, um . . . I mean, I know about drag queens. Are you one of them? Are you gay? Sorry if that's rude. I'm only twelve.

It took me two whole days to send that note, because I was so scared, but Alexis wrote back right away.

Yes! To both things. :) Although it's a bit more complicated than that. . . . Is that why you came to me for advice? Not rude—I've seen rude in my life and that's not it! I remember twelve, long time ago for me.

Yeah. I'm glad I did. :)

Alexis's dream was to be an actor, but she was working at the Copacabana Restaurant downtown for now. She had moved away from home young, because her parents didn't understand her. Then she'd had to run from her evil ex-boyfriend because he wanted to control her. She'd had a hard life but was still happy. And she was so brave. I wanted to be brave like her; I wanted to tell Kayla how I felt and maybe, one day, tell my family the truth too. But I wasn't sure I'd ever be able to do it. It was my dream, just like Alexis and her acting. It's what I wanted more than anything, but my family was the only thing I had.

One night, I saw Alexis talking to someone in her

room, making wild movements with her arms, crying. I quickly scribbled a note and sent it.

Are you okay?

Oh yes! I'm up for a small part in a play and I'm practicing. Sorry if I worried you.

Good luck! That's exciting.

Thank you! This role could be my big break and it would pay enough to help me stay here. Fingers crossed. It's all I've ever wanted.

I crossed my fingers and waved with the other hand, and Alexis did the same.

That night, I prayed Alexis would get the part and never have to talk to her evil ex again, and I prayed for the courage to go after the things I wanted like she did. A thought crept into my brain like mean thoughts do sometimes. If Alexis got the part, I wondered if she would leave. A bad feeling washed over me, because I knew I was being selfish. But I didn't want to lose the only person—the only friend—I could be myself around. I shook my head and focused again on hoping for good things for Alexis, even if they made me feel a little bit sad.

I sent a note the next morning, asking when the audition was, but her window was shut and didn't open the rest of the day. She was probably busy or maybe already at the audition, so I didn't think too much about it. There were ten letters to send out to family anyway, so I focused all my energy on that. The next day, I waited and waited, but Alexis never opened her window.

"What's your problem?" one of my brothers asked in his thick accent.

"Worried about my friend," I said.

He rolled his eyes. "You don't have friends."

"Your English is getting really good," I said with a smile.

He blushed and punched my arm softly before running out of our bedroom.

Three days passed and no Alexis. I waited. Every day my mind filled up with thoughts of all the things that could've gone wrong, and my chest felt tight with worry and sadness. Alexis was the first person I could really be myself with and who had big dreams of going to new places, just like me. She deserved those dreams to come true, didn't she?

Then, one night, I heard them: her boots click-clacking toward home. They sounded far away, so far I shouldn't have been able to hear them, but I did. The sound echoed all around me. It was so loud that I wasn't sure how it didn't wake the entire block. The sound got closer and closer and closer until she was here. I ran to the window and saw Alexis walking slowly to her apartment building. I wanted to yell, to send a note right into her high, curly wig, but I didn't want to scare her. She looked like she'd been through something and lost. When she finally got to her apartment, she pushed aside her curtains, turned a lamp on, and gently removed her wig and lashes, then wiped the makeup off her face. I pulled my special paper and pencils out and started a fresh note.

Where were you?

The note fluttered in the sky like a scared bird, just like my feelings. It landed gently on Alexis's fire escape. She saw it and picked it up, wrote something, and then sent it back. She watched me intently as I unfolded the letter and read.

Out of town, I was auditioning for the part. It didn't go well.

I'm so sorry. Are you okay? I wrote back.

I will be, she responded before giving me a tiny wave and closing her curtains.

I bit my lip, wondering if there was anything I could do to help. I sat down on the cold floor of my bedroom, and goose bumps spread on my legs like a line of falling dominoes. I sat there and thought and thought and finally I realized something: there was *one* thing I could do. I could be a friend, just like Alexis had been for me. I wrote another note, a longer one, about all the new things I'd learned and how I'd never known someone else who was like me. Things that I hadn't told anyone in my life but I could tell Alexis because I knew she'd understand. I wrote all the things I was feeling, poured it all out into the letter. Then I sent it off to Alexis and waited.

Alexis disappeared again, for three days this time. At first I worried my letter had upset her somehow, but she hadn't even read it. It was still sitting on her fire escape, waiting for her window to open. Disappointment won out over any hope I'd had that she would come back or that my note would help. But on the third night, I heard her boots, running this time, and my heart leapt with both happiness and worry. She was running *fast*. I ran to my window just as she reached the front door of her building. I threw my window open so she'd see me, and Alexis smiled the biggest, most beautiful smile I'd ever seen.

"FLOR!" she yelled. It was the first time I could hear her deep, smooth voice clearly.

I looked behind me just in case. My family had the TV turned up loud in the living room, and people yelled outside our building at all hours of the night, but still, I hoped they wouldn't come see what I was up to.

"I WAS WRONG! I GOT THE PART! I DID IT!" She jumped up and down as I climbed onto the fire escape, waving my arms wildly and screaming, not caring if I woke up the whole entire world. Alexis was so happy and so I was happy too. I knew that she would be too busy to write to me all the time now, and I would miss her, but none of that mattered as much as how big her smile was right now. Plus, maybe she would let me dog-sit Rufio.

She read my letter later that night and sent a note back, with just three lines.

Thank you for being my friend. You are wonderful and you are perfect, without conditions, just as you are. Thank you for being you.

I climbed into bed, clutching that note to my chest, and fell asleep knowing what I would do tomorrow. The next morning, I grabbed my extra-special paper, the one with lots of colors and little hearts, and wrote a new note to Kayla. The last one had been too long, and confusing, and now I knew what I wanted to say.

Kayla, it's Flor from class. I like you a lot. Like, like you. Please tell me if you feel the same.

I sealed the letter and kissed it softly, just in case, then sent it and hoped and hoped.

Then I sent another letter to Alexis.

I sent her the letter.

Alexis did an elegant, queen-like clap at her window and nodded approvingly.

Good for you! What changed?

I smiled as I wrote back.

The time was right. In my heart. :)

Kayla wrote back the next day. I saw the pink paper plane land on my windowsill and I opened it so fast I almost got a paper cut. The moment I read her words, I tore the paper into pieces, but it kept putting itself back together. Over and over and over, no matter how many times I tried to make the note go away, it wouldn't. I cried as I read the note.

Sorry.

Just *sorry.* I was so embarrassed and angry that when my mother walked into my room, I wasn't thinking straight. I decided to tell her.

"Mami," I said softly. She smiled at me, and I was scared for a moment that her smile would fade when I said the truth out loud. I was worried she wouldn't smile at me the same way again.

"What's wrong?" my mother asked. Her English was hard to understand, but she was trying and getting better. I was proud of my mami, and I wanted her to be proud of me. *Please, please, please, let her be proud.*

Maybe she could tell how upset I was, because she sat on the bed that two of my brothers shared and patted the spot next to her. I walked over, a few steps that felt like infinity to take, and I sat with my mom.

And then I just said it like it was no big deal.

"I . . . like Kayla, from school, and she told me she doesn't like me back." I looked up at my mami and waited, holding my breath. I really hoped I hadn't just made a giant mistake.

My mother was quiet at first and just stared at me, but then she took my hand and pulled me close and hugged me. She hugged me tightly as I cried and cried, about Kayla and about letting go and about being free. A flower, pink and purple and blue, bloomed in my mother's hand, and she placed it softly behind my ear.

"Te quiero mucho, mucho, mucho. Tal como eres," my mom said, and kissed my wet cheeks with every word. *I love you a lot, a lot, a lot,* she had said. *Just as you are.*

"I love you too, Mami," I said. I was finally free.

That night, after a long talk with my family about everything, during which they told me they loved me no matter what and I felt happier than I ever had, I sent another note to Alexis.

Thank you for helping me be me. Thank you for being you.

Petra & Pearl

BY LISA BUNKER

I AM REALLY close to deciding something, but I just want to go over it all again one more time before I go downstairs (if I don't chicken out) and say things that, once I say them, I can never unsay.

How far back do I need to go? One answer is, all the way back to when I was born. Because I can see, more clearly all the time, that I was born the way I am. So was Pearl. We are who we are, no matter what anyone else believes or says. But I guess, really, to explain the situation, last summer is far enough.

What happened over the summer was that for a while we were so busy doing family summer things that we lost track of getting me haircuts. My hair kept getting longer, and I liked it. I would find myself in the bathroom looking at myself in the mirror, turning my head different ways and tilting it back so my hair touched my shoulders and the back of my neck. It felt really good to me.

Eventually, Mom started talking about how it was high time we went to the barber, and I put her off all the different ways I could think of. I did distractions, and jokes. When she said, "But it's getting so long," I said, "What if I like it?" Which was not the same as actually saying I liked it, but I didn't feel ready to actually say that out loud.

One day when she said that for sure this was the day we were going to do it, I even pretended to be sick. Then she forgot about trying again, and by the end of the summer my hair was touching my shoulders and the back of my neck without me tilting my head back, and I liked it more and more. The day when it was mostly long enough to pull back with a hair tie and make a stubby little ponytail, I cried, all alone in the bathroom with the door locked. And by then, I was beginning to understand why.

The reason that I was beginning to understand why was Pearl. Pearl and I met last year. We both wrote fanfic on the same site about the same two characters in the same show, *Kimazui*—only the best anime program no one has ever heard of in the world. We did beta reads of each other's stories, and that led to a video chat, which lead to another, until it was a regular thing, once a week on Sunday afternoon. Sunday afternoon for me, late Sunday night for her, because she lives in England, which is five hours ahead of us.

And pretty soon, since one of the characters we both wrote about was a trans girl, and since we had both signed on to the fanfic site with girl names, we started talking around the edges of the idea of transness, and for a while neither of us actually said the words, but the idea was in the air. We had intense discussions about our trans characters. We had long conversations about Theory, with both of us being careful to only talk about people in general, not ourselves in particular.

And then, toward the end of the summer, she did say the words. I remember that conversation pretty much exactly.

"Petra, are you ready for my grand, important announcement?" she said, out of nowhere. Pearl's default setting is total drama. Every little thing that happens, she describes like it's either the best thing ever or the end of the world.

"You have a big announcement?"

"Yes, I do."

"Okay, tell me."

"Drumroll, please! I've realized that I am transgender. And I've decided that, as soon as I can, I'm going to be Pearl in my regular life, not just here with you."

"Wow! That's totally amazing! I'm so proud of you!"

I said. As soon as the words came out of my mouth, I thought they sounded weird, but she liked it.

"Thank you," she whispered, and ducked her head, which is what she does when she's being bashful.

"What about your parents? From what you've told me about them, they might not react very well."

"I said 'as soon as I can.' I don't know yet when that might be."

"Well, I'm honored that you told me first. And I think you're awesome and beautiful."

She ducked her head again. "Thank you very much," she said.

Then there was a silence that felt like my chance to say the words too, but I couldn't. I wasn't sure yet, or not ready, or something. So it was awkward for a second, but we got past it by going back to talking about Theory. Pearl does a lot of reading online, and she has taught me all sorts of stuff, about Patriarchy and Privilege and Transphobia—all these amazing new words.

When I told her she was beautiful, it was not in an I-want-to-date-you way, just in a being-a-good-friend way. Pearl is my friend. Actually, right now, she is my only real friend. I mean, I have friends, but this weird gap has opened up between us, because this thing is happening, and none of them know about it. And I guess they can't be super-close friends, because when I pulled away, no one asked why. They just let me go off alone. So for a while now, Pearl has been the only one I can talk to.

The other thing that happened near the end of the summer was the fight I had with my dad. The thing about my dad is, he's sure that he's right about everything, all the time. It's in how he holds his face, and it comes out in his voice, too. I mean, besides what he says, obviously. My point is, it's not just his words, it's how he says them. Instead of asking, he tells.

Or assumes. That's how it went when it was time to pick classes for this year. We were talking about how school was beginning again soon, and he was going on about how cool it was that I would be taking shop from Mr. Sullivan, who is a friend of his, and he wasn't saying *if,* he was saying *when.*

Which I suppose makes sense in a way, because they're friends, and because Dad builds houses for a living, so there has always been this idea that I was going to learn everything I could about building things. But he must have seen something of what I was feeling on my face, because he stopped in the middle of a sentence and said, "What? What's the matter?"

That was hard to answer, and not just because he's always hard to answer. It was because I hadn't had a chance yet to put my thoughts into words. It was just the instant strong feeling of not wanting to take shop.

Especially from Mr. Sullivan, who is also a PE teacher and who likes his boys all macho and tough, like him. I had him for PE last year, and that was no fun, I can tell you. I'm tall—taller than I'd like to be—but I'm not an athlete, and I guess even before I started growing my hair long, I seemed kinda girlish to people like him. He never said anything in actual words, but his voice always had this sound of disgust or sarcasm in it, and when some of his boy-boys picked on me, he made sure not to notice.

Anyway, there I was with my mouth open and my face feeling hot, and Dad said, "Of course you're taking shop. What else could you possibly take?"

"Art," I thought, but didn't say. I also didn't say, "And I want to be a techie again for the fall play." I really liked that. Returning students sometimes get to do set design, and Mrs. Johnson is so much nicer to be around.

"It's not an open question," Dad said. "You're taking shop, and you're going to like it." Mom made a little sound when he said that, but he gave her one of his I-know-everything looks, and she bowed her head and didn't make any more sounds. She always caves when his face goes hard like that.

I do too. At least, I always have until now.

Anyway, I ended up in shop, no surprise there, and it took about three seconds for Trent and Mike and those guys to start picking on me. "Nice haircut, loser," Trent said as soon as he saw me. "You look like a girl." Which was weird to hear coming from him, because I was starting to feel more and more sure that I was a girl—*am* a girl—but I couldn't say that to him. So I just kept my head down and did my best to ignore them, the way I always do.

Then they threw wood chips at me, and Mike dumped sawdust in my hair, and of course Mr. Sullivan pretended not to notice. And there was no one in the class I liked or who liked me even a little. No one who might have said something. So that's how it has been ever since.

Oh, and one more thing: they decided to give me a girl name. They started calling me Sally. With their voices all sarcastic, of course. At first it was just in shop class, but then it started spreading around school. People started pulling on my ponytail, too. It has been a tough year for that kind of stupid stuff, every day.

I didn't actually mind them giving me a girl name. I was just annoyed because it wasn't the name I wanted. Not that I could say that out loud, either.

Anyway, like I said, Pearl and I usually talk on Sundays, but I keep the app open, and last week on Tuesday night I got a surprise call from her. It was right at my bedtime, so it was the middle of the night for her, and when her screen came up, I could see that her whole room was dark except for one little desk lamp with its cone turned toward the wall. The video of her face was all grainy and crawly, the way it gets when there isn't enough light, but she also looked zombie-faced too, because of the white light from her screen. And she whispered so low I could hardly hear her, and what she said was, "Oh, thank God you're there."

"Hey, Pearl. What's going on?"

"My life is over."

Like I said before, it's all drama all the time with Pearl, so I stayed calm and used one of the little phrases I've figured out to invite her to talk more. That's what friends do, right? "Yeah, what's up?"

"I was playing with my sister's clothes, you know, and my sister walked in on me, because I guess I forgot to lock the door, and she told my mum, and my mum told my dad, and there was a horrible row."

"Whoa," I said.

"But that's not all. When my dad was shouting at me, calling me all these horrible names, all of a sudden I got super mad, and I shouted back at him, and what I shouted was that I'm trans and I want to be called Pearl from now on."

"Whoa!" I said. I knew from other talks since she came out to me that she had been planning to wait, maybe a long time, before coming out to her family. They're really conservative. Also, they're pretty poor and her dad just lost his job, so things look bad for the whole family. This was not the best time to spring a big surprise on them like that.

"And now I'm locked in my room and can hear my dad still shouting, and I don't know what they're going to do, and I'm afraid." Pearl started to cry.

Hearing her talk about how her dad was being, of course it made me imagine how my dad might react if I told him the same thing, and I started to shake. But by now my friend was sobbing, so I tried my hardest to push away my own fear and just keep talking to her. We went back and forth for a while, her imagining the horrible things that might happen, and me trying to calm her down and keep her company. After a while we started going over stuff for the second time, and it had gotten late, so I said as gently as I could that it was time for me to go to sleep. "Are you going to be okay?" I asked her, and she looked at me with tears on her cheeks and said, "I don't know," and ended the call. No "Thanks for talking," no "Bye." Just, boom, done.

So I went to sleep and woke up again and went to school, and I kept thinking about that call and worrying about my friend. That night I tried to call her. No answer. It went on like that for the rest of the week—no answer, no answer—and I didn't have any other way to get in touch with her, so I started to get really worried. Even on Sunday night, no answer. And I couldn't talk about it with anyone. I had to carry around this horrible feeling that maybe my secret friend in England was in terrible trouble, and I couldn't find anything out, and I couldn't help. It sucked so bad.

Then this morning in shop, Trent came over and pushed my birdhouse onto the floor so that it broke, and then he said, real mean, "Gonna cry now, Sally?" I looked over at Mr. Sullivan, and he just looked back at me like, "I'm not going to help you at all." Then I had this weird idea that I was seeing my father's head on Mr. Sullivan's body, and I guess I snapped, because these words just started pouring out of me, words I learned from Pearl: Bigot, Sexist, Toxic Masculinity. I chewed out my teacher in front of the whole class. At first Mr. Sullivan looked puzzled, then surprised. Then his face went stone hard, and when I saw that, I suddenly thought, "What in heaven's name am I doing?" That's another thing Pearl says: "What in heaven's name?" So then I blushed really hard and stopped in the middle of a sentence, and everyone was staring, and Trent and Mike and those guys were laughing, and I just wanted to sink down through the floor and disappear. Then Mr. Sullivan sent me to see Ms. Cooper, and I got suspended.

So now I'm home, in my room, waiting for my dad

to come home. I feel embarrassed and scared, but there's another thing too, a kind of wild excitement, like the feeling you get when you're standing in line waiting to ride a humongous roller coaster. All these powerful feelings, all at once. It's super uncomfortable.

Then one more thing happened, just a couple of minutes ago. My computer chimed, and it was Pearl. Of course I clicked right away, and there she was, with a different room behind her. "Thank God!" I said. "I am so glad to see you! Are you okay?"

I was expecting the usual drama, but she seemed weirdly calm. Calm, but sad. "Petra, it has been a horrible time," she said. "But I'm a little better now."

"What happened?"

"My dad said he was going to kick me out of the house—"

"Oh, Pearl, no!"

"—if I didn't take it back, but I said I couldn't take it back."

"So did he kick you out?"

"Almost. My mum begged him not to do anything rash, and they locked me in my room again while they argued some more, and finally they decided to send me to stay with my granny in Leeds until they could figure out what to do."

"You mean, like, you live there now?"

She sighed and wiped at the corner of one eye with the heel of her hand. "I don't know. I don't think so."

"And have they decided what they're going to do?"

"No." She stared off to the side for a second, then looked back at me. "The last I heard, my granny said my mum called and that they're still trying to figure it out." She wiped her eye again. "At least no one is shouting anymore. And my granny is pretty okay, for an old person. They told her why they asked her to take me, but she didn't say anything, she just did this *tut-tut* thing she does. Her house smells funny, and I don't like her food all that much, but at least I feel almost safe."

"That sounds about as good as it could be, considering the circumstances," I said, and Pearl nodded. There was a silence. Then I said, "I got suspended from school today."

"Really? Why?"

So then I told her the story about snapping at Mr. Sullivan, and when I got to the part about chewing him out, she laughed. I was happy to hear that, because I figured if she could laugh, it meant she was really feeling better. "That's cracking! Good on you!" she said.

"Thanks," I said. I felt better hearing her say that. I felt like, you know, I really do have someone on my side. Whatever is about to happen next, I need to remember that.

"Petra, I have to go," Pearl said. "But before I do, I want to thank you."

I was surprised by that, and said, "Thank me? For what?"

"It was really bad that first night. I thought I was going to get kicked out, and I felt like maybe I should run away first. But then when I called you, you were there, and you listened, and I felt a little better, because it helped me remember that I'm not alone in the world. I've got you. You're a true friend. So, thank you for being there when I needed someone."

"I was just thinking the exact same thing!" I said, half laughing, half crying. She was emotional too, and for a second we just sat there grinning at each other and wiping our eyes. Then we both said, *Okay, good luck, hang in there, yeah, you too,* and ended the call.

Since then, I've been sitting here thinking, and what I've been thinking is, I've been feeling sorry for myself and afraid to talk to my parents, especially my dad, but you know what? Compared to Pearl, compared to a lot of people, I have it easy. My parents both have jobs, and we have, I don't know about plenty of money, but I feel like we have enough, which is more than it sounds like Pearl can say. And my dad can be so stubborn sometimes, so sure that he's right, but I don't think he would kick me out of the house. At least, I hope not.

Anyway, it doesn't matter, because I know now. I know who I am. And it's time to say.

I didn't put much thought at all into my fanfic name. When I signed on to the site for the first time, I had just watched a movie with a character named Petra in it, and I liked it, so I used it. I've gotten used to it now, though, and there's one person in the world—Pearl—who has never known me by any other name. So, that's who I am.

I'm Petra.

When my dad gets home, there's going to be a talk, and I'm going to let my parents say whatever they think they have to say, and when it's my turn, I'm going to say, "Mom, Dad, I have two things I need to tell you." And they're going to say, "What are the two things?" And I am going to say, "The first one is, I'm dropping shop."

I Know the Way

BY JUSTINA IRELAND

THE CORN BREAD had burned.

Addie knew it as soon as Cora pulled the loaf from the woodstove. The acrid scent of charred bread filled the summer kitchen and made Addie's whole body clench with dread.

"You burned it," she whispered quietly, so Sylvie, the kitchen's overseer, wouldn't hear. Sylvie had a quick temper and an even quicker hand, and a pan of burnt corn bread would earn both.

Cora's bottom lip trembled, still swollen from the last time Sylvie had backhanded her. Addie had worked in the kitchens for most of her twelve summers, but Cora was new, bought only a fortnight ago, and her mistakes seemed to pile up more and more quickly each day. Addie liked Cora well enough—the girl was good at making games out of boring work—but not enough to take the whip for her.

"Here, you take that out to the hogpen. I'll put in a new batch," Addie said, her heart thumping painfully. "But you gotta run, you hear me? And make sure no one sees you." If Sylvie found out, it would be both their hides.

Cora nodded and grabbed the cast-iron pan, lighting out across the open yard and scattering chickens as she went. Addie began mixing ingredients as quickly as she could so that she could dump fresh batter in the pan and put it all back in the woodstove before Sylvie found out. As she mixed, she swallowed dryly.

Maybe it would be okay.

EVELYN SAT IN HER SOCIAL STUDIES CLASS and swallowed a jaw-cracking yawn. She was fighting to stay awake in the too-warm classroom and only half listening to the never-ending lecture on early American settlers. Her teacher, Mrs. Howard, was talking about how the colonists who had settled Maryland lived, and Evelyn did not care in the least about the dusty old first Marylanders.

"I know a lot of this seems archaic and weird, but I promise it'll make more sense once we see the settlement at Jerusalem Mill. It will be a bit more exciting when you get to see it for yourself," Mrs. Howard said.

"We're going on a field trip?" someone asked, and the classroom exploded in excitement, everyone talking at once.

"Jerusalem Mill sucks," said Ashley, the girl who sat next to Evelyn. "We went there three years ago, and it's nothing but a farm and some guy making pottery."

"The chickens are cool, though," Evelyn said with a small smile. She'd gone to Jerusalem Mill in fourth grade as well, and she'd liked how strange and weird it had seemed. Plus, it wasn't that far from Gunpowder Falls, which was a really cool stream.

"Yeah, and if we go, maybe we'll see a ghost," said Jennifer, leaning forward to join the conversation. "You know, the bridge there is haunted."

"Haunted?" Ashley said, her brows pulling together in a way that Evelyn liked entirely too much. She'd been watching Ashley since the beginning of the school year, and had made a mental list of her expressions that she liked. The small frown was high on the list.

"Yeah, the story is that they used to hang runaway slaves from the rafters as a warning to the other slaves in the area to not run away. And then, during the Civil War, they hung soldiers who tried to run away from the same rafters. If you go and you see the ghosts, all you see are their feet dangling."

"That's awful," Evelyn said. She hated when people

talked about slavery. She always felt like people expected her to feel some kind of way about it because she was one of the only Black girls in school. It mostly just made her angry, and how was that useful?

"But ghosts!" Ashley said. "I want to see that."

"Did you girls have a question?" Mrs. Howard cut in, silencing any further speculation about ghosts and making Evelyn sink lower in her seat. Ashley gave her a goofy look, and Evelyn swallowed a laugh.

But the more Evelyn thought about it, the more she wanted to try to find the ghosts. And the more she wanted to find them with Ashley.

ADDIE PULLED THE SECOND CORN BREAD from the oven. It was perfectly golden yellow, exactly as it should have been. Addie began to mix another batch while Cora watched, sullen and quiet.

"Why we got to be scared of a little burnt corn bread?" the girl asked, arms crossed.

Addie glanced at Cora as she put another pan in the oven. It was blazing out, and she wiped the sweat from her brow with the back of her sleeve. "You stop burning it and you ain't gonna have nothing to be scared of."

Cora shook her head, and looked out of the summer

kitchen and across the yard. There were two other kitchens on Bent Creek Plantation, plus a smokehouse and a
weaving house, but most everyone was out in the tobacco
fields, so not another soul was about. That was the only
reason Cora had been able to so easily hide her error. On
any other day, the yard would have been bustling, and
someone would have told Sylvie.

"We should run away."

Addie paused in her stirring and looked up at Cora.
"You keep talking like that and you're gonna be best
friends with Sylvie's backhand and the whip besides."

"You ain't ever thought about it? Running away?"

"Nope," Addie said, filling yet another pan with corn
bread batter so that it would be ready to go in the oven
when the other one came out. Since Cora didn't look like
she was going to help, Addie had set to the work by herself. "There's dogs, and I saw what happened to Big Bill
when he tried to run off." The memory of the whip carv-
ing bloody lines into the man's back made Addie's stomach clench. She would never forget the sounds of the big
man's sobbing, but that hadn't made the master let up
any. He'd still given Bill a full fifty lashes.

"Well, I ain't staying," Cora said, finally coming over
to pull the pan from the oven with a pair of tongs. "I was
free until Johnny Reb snatched me and my family up,
and I can be free again. All I got to do is follow the North

Star like the song says. And eventually I'll get to Pennsylvania and freedom."

Addie didn't say anything, just kept stirring batter and pouring it into empty pans.

If Cora was going to be a fool, she could be one by herself.

EVELYN DIDN'T KNOW EXACTLY WHEN SHE'D

started noticing the things about Ashley, like the way her hair curled around her hairline, or the way her cheeks pinkened when she was excited, but over the past few months Evelyn's feelings toward her friend had grown to be something prickly and heated. Evelyn wanted to hold Ashley's hand, wanted to tell her about all of the things she felt. But that seemed like a lot, so she pushed aside the feelings and tried to ignore them.

It didn't work.

She thought maybe Ashley liked her too. Didn't she send her funny GIFs and silly animal videos every day? No one texted Evelyn as much as Ashley did, and Evelyn found each text more endearing than the last. Even when her mother yelled at her that screen time was over and she had to put her phone away, she had a little smile each time the phone dinged with another message from Ashley.

So she'd had the idea that they could sneak away and find the ghosts, just the two of them. Maybe then, if Evelyn told Ashley how she felt, the strange shaken-can-of-soda-pop feeling in her middle would go away. Evelyn hadn't told anyone her plan, and she thought it was probably stupid, but every time Ashley said something nice to her, the anxious feeling grew a little.

And Ashley had lots of nice things to say to Evelyn.

"I love your hair like that!" she said, bouncing into class the day of the field trip, her dark hair pulled up into twin pigtails that made Evelyn smile.

"It's just cornrows," Evelyn said, her voice quiet. "You could wear them too."

Ashley laughed. "No, I cannot. There is nothing worse than white people wearing cornrows," she said, plopping down next to Evelyn. "Have you heard of cultural appropriation?"

Evelyn shook her head, and Ashley launched into a lecture about how people took things from other cultures in a way that removed the significance or got praise while the original group got shamed. Evelyn was fascinated. Ashley was always saying smart things, and she learned a lot by listening to the other girl, even if she mostly just liked hearing her talk.

They were sitting outside, waiting to board the bus, and the teachers and chaperones for the field trip were still trying to figure out who was going where. Jennifer was off talking to a group of boys who were jumping up and trying to touch the sign above the door into the school. Suddenly Mrs. Howard clapped her hands.

"Okay, when I read your name, you're going to get on the bus. The person you sit next to is your partner," the teacher said. Evelyn's heart sank. Her last name was Thomas and Ashley's was Miller. No way they would be next to each other.

Ashley groaned. "I do not want to sit next to Bret Miller. He smells like feet."

But it was too late. Mrs. Howard was calling names, and Ashley gave Evelyn a sad little wave as she boarded the bus and sat down. Now what was she going to do? Her one chance to spend time with Ashley, maybe have an adventure together, was gone.

An Asian girl Evelyn didn't know plopped down next to her and immediately pulled out her phone. Evelyn didn't even bother trying to say hi. She could take a hint.

CORA DID NOT LET UP ON HER TALK OF running away. For the next few days she brought it up at every opportunity, so that Addie grew sick of hearing about heading north and the many different ways Cora was planning on running away.

She finally lost her temper with the girl one morning as they fed the chickens. "If'n you want to run, run, but stop talking about it. I'm sick of hearing about it."

Cora shook all her seed out so that it fell in a pile, exactly like Addie had told her not to do a number of times. The girl was as thick as a slab of salt pork. "You should come with me."

"No, I ain't a fool."

Cora put her hands on her hips. "What are you afraid of?"

Addie thought of all that she knew about people who had tried to run away, the whippings, the beatings, the dogs that the slave patrol used. "Everything."

Cora grabbed Addie's hand, causing her to drop a good measure of seed into a pile at her feet, the chickens rushing one another to get to the treasure. Addie barely noticed, her focus on the feeling of her hand in Cora's. She liked it a bit too much.

"If we go together, it's safer," she said. "Come with me. I know the way."

"How do you know the way when you've never left the farm?" Addie demanded, pulling her hand away and placing it on her hip.

"You've just got to follow the North Star! Plus, there's a map in the old man's study. I can figure out which way to go from that." Cora refused to call the master by his proper title; instead, she called him "the old man" or "a no-good Confederate."

"What's a map got to do with anything?" Addie asked.

"It has directions, and I can read them when we run. So we won't get lost."

A strange feeling came over Addie, part hope and part jealousy. "You can read?"

"Yep! My mama taught me." Cora got quiet, and her expression went from excited to sad for a moment before she righted it. "I could teach you how to read, too! All we need is a Bible—that's how I learned. As soon as we get to Pennsylvania, I'll get one and teach you."

"Fine, I'll go," Addie found herself saying, not quite sure how the girl had talked her into such a stupid move. She should stay on the plantation, just mind her own business. But being able to read seemed like something magical, and if Cora could do magic, maybe they could make it to freedom after all.

Maybe, with Cora by her side, she could be brave.

THE DRIVE TO JERUSALEM MILL WASN'T that long, and when they piled out of the bus, Evelyn walked, her shoulders hunched, to where Mrs. Howard was yelling at them to gather. Her partner disappeared into a crush of bodies, so when Evelyn joined her class, she couldn't see where the girl had gone.

"Does everyone have their partners?" Mrs. Howard asked.

Evelyn didn't want to get yelled at, so she said nothing, just stood a little awkwardly by herself. Ashley saw her and slipped away from Bret's side.

"Where'd your partner go?" she asked.

Evelyn shrugged. "I don't know."

Ashley scowled, and before she could say anything, Evelyn grabbed her hand. "Ditch smelly old Bret and be my partner."

Ashley's scowl faded and was replaced by a slow smile. "Great idea."

Evelyn's heart thumped painfully with joy, and she nodded, releasing the other girl's hand. The soda-pop feeling left her belly and went straight to her head. She'd done something she never normally would, and it had worked out okay.

Maybe she could be a little bold. Not like Ashley, but in her own kind of way.

Mrs. Howard finished her lecture. They had until lunchtime to explore as they liked. After lunch, there would be some demonstrations and a tour of the village. Ashley wasted no time in grabbing Evelyn's hand, setting off a fresh round of effervescence in Evelyn's belly.

"Come on, let's go find those ghosts."

ADDIE REGRETTED TELLING CORA THAT SHE would run away with her as soon as the words left her mouth, but there was no taking them back. She wasn't the kind of girl to break a promise, and she wouldn't start.

Because now that she was thinking about the possibility of running, she found herself preoccupied with the idea more than she liked. She thought about it as she carried water up to the main house for washing, and as she emptied the dirty water out near the privy. She thought about it while kneading bread and picking berries down near the creek.

So when Cora jostled her slightly a few nights later, Addie was already awake and ready to go. Cora motioned for her to be quiet, and she nodded. Then they were tiptoeing past Sylvie and the others in the women's cabin, out into the chilly stillness of the night.

The moon was high, but thick clouds scudded across the sky, making it hard to see the North Star. And yet there it was, just like the songs said.

"You got the map?" Addie asked, following instead of leading for once.

"Don't need it. I memorized the route. Come on." Cora took her hand, calming down the angry-bee buzz of fear in Addie's middle just a bit.

They tiptoed on silent feet until they were past the farthest edge of the plantation, and then Cora pulled Addie along. They ran through woods that sloped and dipped, and everything was going better than Addie had expected.

A giddiness filled her, lifting her up. Was this what hope felt like? She actually believed in that moment that maybe, maybe she and Cora could find their freedom by way of the North Star.

Maybe Cora really would buy Addie that Bible and teach her how to read.

But then a rock shifted under Addie's foot, tricking her ankle into twisting the wrong way. She tried to catch herself and right her balance, but the ground was not where she expected it to be, and she fell headlong down the hill.

THEY WEREN'T SUPPOSED TO LEAVE THE
Jerusalem Mill village proper, so Evelyn knew as soon
as they ducked around the last stand of buildings that
there was a good chance they'd get in trouble if they were
caught. But Ashley's hand was warm in hers, and Evelyn
couldn't seem to find the fear of punishment that normally kept her from breaking the rules. Ashley had a way
of making those sorts of things seem unimportant.

"Where is the bridge from here?" Evelyn asked, trying not to pull back her hand. As long as Ashley wanted
to keep their sweaty fingers twined together, she would.

"This way. I went hiking with my mom once. But
we're going to have to run, otherwise we won't make it
back in time for lunch."

And then they were flying down a rocky hiking path
to the bridge. Evelyn wasn't athletic by any measure, but
holding Ashley's hand seemed to give her an extra boost.
They ran, skipping over rocks and laughing as squirrels
darted out of their path. And then they rounded a corner
and there was the bridge.

It was a covered bridge, and it looked like someone
had decided to build a barn over the creek. Evelyn had
expected something more impressive, but the bridge was
almost utterly forgettable.

"This is it?" she asked, trying to keep from sounding
unhappy.

"Yeah. Wait, you've really never seen the bridge?" Ashley asked.

"No, last time we came here, we weren't supposed to go this far down the path." Evelyn did not point out that they weren't supposed to go this far down the path this time, either.

"Oh," Ashley said, disappointment in her voice. "I thought you wanted to come to the bridge because . . ." She trailed off, and then shook her head. She dropped Evelyn's hand suddenly. "Never mind. Let me show you where the ghosts are supposed to be."

THE AIR WHOOSHED OUT OF ADDIE AS SHE

went, leaves and a few rocks catching her as she tumbled end over end. She came to a stop flat on her back, heart pounding, panic making her head light.

"You all right?" Cora whisper-yelled.

"Yes," Addie said, staying where she lay as she gathered her wits. For a moment, she thought she'd hit her head—her eyes were dazzled by strange lights. But then she realized they were far-off lanterns bobbing through the night.

"Cora!"

"I see them," the other girl said, ducking down next to where Addie had landed.

"Do you think they're after us?" Addie asked, sitting up.

"No, look, they're up on the road. They're heading toward the bridge."

They watched as a group of men walked by, talking loudly. They carried guns but they didn't look like a slave patrol. Addie had always heard that the patrols ran with dogs. Still, the men looked dangerous. As they got to the bridge, they laughed, pointing to something inside. What could be so funny?

"Johnny Reb," Cora said, spitting for luck. "We'll stay here until they get past." The tremor in her voice was the only thing to reveal her fear. "Be brave, Addie. Be brave!"

They stayed down among the rocks and the leaves for a long moment as the group wandered off, the sound of their passage easily traceable in the still night, then they made their own careful way up toward the road and the bridge. A powerful stink came to them, like meat gone bad, and Cora grabbed Addie's arm as they walked.

"Look!" she whispered.

Dangling above them were men in strange blue uniforms, their faces bloated and ropes around their necks.

Addie didn't hesitate. She grabbed Cora's hand and they started running once more, Cora's words—*be brave be brave*—a mantra she sang in time to their footsteps.

She would run all the way to freedom rather than go back.

And so, with Cora's hand in hers, she did.

ASHLEY STOOD IN THE MIDDLE OF THE bridge and pointed up. "See, that's where they used to hang the soldiers from," she said.

Evelyn couldn't quite force herself to walk over the bridge. Everything in her seemed to clench up with fear. Ashley frowned at her from where she stood. "Ev, you scared?"

Evelyn was terrified. Not just of the possibility of ghosts but of everything else besides. Of getting in trouble for running off, of the way Ashley made her feel, of everything. How could she tell this wild girl how she made her heart thump nearly as much as the thought of ghosts?

Be brave be brave be brave, came a whisper. Evelyn whipped her head around to look for the speaker, but she and Ashley were alone.

Evelyn took a deep breath and stood next to Ashley on the bridge. "Do you like me?"

"Uh, yeah. Why are you even asking?" Ashley said, brows knit together in confusion.

Evelyn's heart pounded in her ears. "No, I don't mean as friends. I mean *like* like," she said.

Ashley's cheeks went ruddy, and she yanked her hand out of Evelyn's. "Yeah, I do. Sorry."

Evelyn grinned and grabbed for Ashley's hand. "Why are you apologizing?"

Ashley blinked. "What, do you mean you like me, too?"

Evelyn smiled and nodded, and before she knew what was happening, Ashley pulled her forward and planted a quick kiss on her lips. "I'm glad," she said. "I was afraid you didn't."

Be brave.

Evelyn smiled and gave Ashley a kiss back.

That was when they heard the yelling.

"Oh, we are going to be in so much trouble," Ashley laughed. Then she grabbed Evelyn's hand and pulled her along, the two of them running hand in hand all the way back.

Balancing Acts

BY A. J. SASS

KAI STANDS IN front of the gym's double doors. The welcome sign stares back, with its familiar, multicolored letters. A new poster hangs beside it, advertising today's gymnastics meet. Kai studies it as a family of four approaches from the parking lot.

The man reaches for the closest door.

"Use the other," Kai offers. "That one sticks."

Or it used to. Maybe it's been fixed in the months since eir last visit.

"Thank you." The woman smiles at Kai as her husband opens the other door. The kids scamper through it.

Kai could leave now. Turn around, go home, and text Jaycie that e couldn't make it. But what about the next meet she invites em to, and the next? E can't stand the thought of being so close, yet never quite able to rip off the Band-Aid and return to the gym to cheer on eir old teammates.

So Kai steels emself and follows the family toward the stands, shoulders rounded and hands shoved in both pockets.

The gym is alive with energy as gymnasts warm up on each of four apparatuses. It's an electric prickle in Kai's legs each time e hears the squeak of the vault springboard, a tingle in eir arms when e passes a girl swinging on the uneven bars.

Kai takes a quick look around, but there's no sign anyone notices em. E lets out a breath and climbs into the stands, choosing a seat hidden among the other spectators as the meet begins.

Kai's gaze skitters from one piece of equipment to another, pausing on the balance beam. Eir heart skips a beat as e spots eir old team, but e looks away, not quite ready for the flood of memories.

E watches another team take turns at the vault. Each girl's legs and arms pump as she runs, building momentum. One by one, their feet hit the springboard. Then they're airborne. Flipping, twisting, weightless.

Kai's leg muscles tense. E remembers the split second when the audience fell silent, waiting to see if e'd win the fight to stay upright. The proud flutter in eir chest after a stuck landing. High fives from all of eir teammates.

A knot twists inside of em. E used to be part of this world, celebrating each teammate's success and commiserating when a routine didn't go well. Now e's an outsider looking in. This sport no longer belongs to em.

The Klaxon blares, tinny and loud, signaling the start of the next rotation. Across the gym, a girl swings on the uneven bars. Everyone's eyes are on her, including Kai's as e focuses on the little bursts of chalk dust as the girl releases one bar and catches the other. Relief washes through em and the knot loosens. At least no one's watching em compete anymore, assuming e's a girl.

A second Klaxon blast, and e steals a glance toward a row of balance beams on the other side of the gym. A girl in a shimmery red leotard points her toes with each careful step across the narrow apparatus.

People clap, but Kai doesn't move an inch.

Teams circulate in the gym as the last rotation begins. Finally, Kai lets emself search for the familiar white uniforms with a sparkly blue stripe dividing them down the middle. E spots Jaycie first as she heads toward the floor with the rest of her team. They move in unison, their steps a perfectly timed march.

One by one, Kai's former teammates perform their floor routines. E claps slowly at first as Shannon executes a tricky forward tumbling pass, then faster as Dominique performs intricate choreography right on the beat of the music. By the time Jaycie settles into her opening pose, Kai has become an active member of the audience.

Jaycie performs her routine, chest out, back arched, each movement perfectly choreographed. She's a blur of white and blue that handsprings, twists, and tucks from one corner of the floor to the other.

She pauses before her final pass, and the crowd seems to hold its breath. Her shoulders rise and fall, and then she's off into a roundoff, back handspring, full twisting layout. Kai jumps to eir feet with the rest of the audience as Jaycie grins, then salutes the judges.

The tight feeling in Kai's chest returns as volunteers set up a podium for the medal ceremony. Eir heart beats faster as Jaycie's name is called for bars, vault, and floor. Jaycie accepts a silver medal for the individual all-around, then looks up into the stands.

Their eyes lock, and Kai has the sudden urge to run out of the gym. But it was Jaycie who'd texted, inviting Kai to watch the meet. She'd said she wanted to see em, and deep down Kai wants to see her too. E forces emself to stay seated.

Jaycie's gaze flickers away until the end of the ceremony. The moment it's over, she hops off the podium. Her medals clink together as she takes the stairs up to em.

"You came!"

Kai nods as she stops a couple of steps below em. "You killed it out there, Cie-Cie. The whole team did."

"Thanks. But we missed you." Jaycie lowers her voice. "No one came close to your beam score from last year. You definitely would've medaled."

She acts like she's sharing a secret, even though everyone seated around Kai has already filed down to ground level. Maybe this is good, Kai tells emself. Maybe Cie-Cie finally realizes e doesn't want people to know that eir name used to be longer and whenever people heard it, they automatically thought *girl*.

Still, Kai swallows hard.

I missed you all too, e wants to say. But even if Cie-Cie understands Kai better now, Kai still can't help thinking that she might wonder if e's had second thoughts about quitting the team—because not so long ago, she and Kai's other teammates tried to convince em to stay. They didn't get that changing eir name and pronouns wasn't enough, that if e'd stuck with gymnastics, people would still see em as someone e's not.

"You're playing tennis now?" Cie-Cie asks when Kai stays silent.

"I was." Kai quit last month, but e leaves that part out. "Now I'm taking a digital art class."

"That sounds cool."

"It is."

It's not even close to gymnastics, but at least the kids in eir art class don't get arranged by gender.

Kai pushes the thought away and studies Cie-Cie. She's slicked her hair back into a tight ponytail with glittery hair spray and bouncy curls. Right before the medal ceremony, she slid on athletic pants and her team jacket, but a hint of leotard remains visible above the jacket's zipper.

E slouches at the thought of wearing that uniform again, grateful that eir baggy T-shirt hides eir chest. If only there were a way to be part of the team without sending everyone the wrong message.

Kai knows there isn't.

"The meet was fun to watch," e says, which isn't a lie but it's not the whole truth either. "Especially your floor routine. That final pass, Cie-Cie. Just, *wow*. I didn't even know you were working on a full twisting layout."

"Thanks." Cie-Cie's face breaks out into the same big smile she wore when saluting the judges. "Coach started me on it this spring after you . . . you know."

Another twinge. Kai had tried tennis to fill the hole left by quitting gymnastics. But girls wear different uniforms than boys in tennis too, and Kai wouldn't have known which one to choose. Same for the swim team eir younger sister, Lexi, tried to get em to join. Digital art is an activity that finally allows Kai to just be Kai.

Except art class doesn't make eir heart race with excitement, and no one high-fives em after e completes a tricky design project. Sometimes it feels like e's stuck, no matter what e tries.

"You coming, Jaycie?" Dominique calls from the bottom of the stands. "Hi, Kai." Her voice rises like she's speaking a word she just learned in a different language, all uncertain.

"Just a sec." Cie-Cie holds up one hand, then turns back to Kai. "We're going to Cellini's to celebrate. You should come."

Kai looks from Cie-Cie to Dominique, then down at the rest of eir former teammates. Duffel bags are slung over their shoulders. Everyone's ready to head to the team's favorite restaurant. Last year, Kai would've gone too. E'd have laughed at Cie-Cie's mock-grossed-out face as e ordered a slice of pizza topped with pineapple and jalapeño.

Now all e wants is to avoid having to explain emself for the thousandth time. The team is all girls. A boy wouldn't want to be on their team, and neither does Kai.

E pulls out eir phone and pretends to look at the time.

"Can't. I promised I'd get Lexi from her friend's house and walk her home."

That's another half-truth, since Lexi isn't expecting em for a while yet. But this isn't eir world anymore, so neither are post-meet hangouts.

"Oh." Cie-Cie frowns. She hops down a few steps, toward Dominique. "Well, thanks for coming to watch. Text me later?"

"Sure, yeah."

Kai doesn't climb down from the stands until all eir former teammates are out the door. Then e takes each step as slowly as possible. Now that e's not practicing with the team anymore, e wants to savor every moment left in the gym.

"Well, hey!" E whirls in place, but it's only the gym's owner, Maxine. She stands in front of the main office door, a spray bottle and cloth in her hands. "It's been a minute since I last saw you around here. Coach Landis mentioned you're going by Kai now?"

Kai nods.

"Short and simple—I like it. And it's nice to see your face around the gym again, even if you just came to watch."

Kai still has time before e has to pick up Lexi. While eir team seems like part of a world e no longer fits neatly

into, the gym feels like coming home after a long vaca-
tion.

"Hey, Maxine? Would it be okay if I stayed? I won't
try anything dangerous, promise. Nothing I'd need
a spotter for. I just, you know . . ." E shrugs and looks
down, not sure how to explain why e misses something e
chose to give up.

"Sure. Of course, kiddo." Maxine's voice is a different
kind of quiet, not embarrassed like Cie-Cie's but gentle
and understanding. "It'd be nice to have some company
while I clean up before the next class. I'll try to keep an
eye on you, but holler if you need anything."

Maxine heads toward the uneven bars. An occa-
sional spritz as she wipes down the wood-coated fiber-
glass is the only sound that breaks the gym's comfortable
quiet.

Kai takes a step into the middle of the gym, between
the floor mats and the tumble track, where kids can
practice acrobatic passes on a bouncier surface. Nothing
much has changed. E scans the entire space, gaze snag-
ging on the row of balance beams.

Kai drifts toward the beams as though drawn by an
invisible string. E remembers how the leathery material
felt under eir feet, and the way eir toes would curl along
either side to steady emself before a leap. E steps in front
of one, then stops, hands balling up tight. The last time

e stood on a beam, people knew em by a different name. One that told everyone Kai was a girl.

No one's around who'd tell em balance beams are only for girls.

E kicks eir shoes off and reaches out to touch the smooth surface. At Kai's final team practice, eir chin was level with the beam. Now e can look down at it a little.

Kai presses up, elbows locking. For a moment, e straddles the beam, imagining the sound of the crowd at a meet mingling with the music of another competitor's floor routine.

E breathes in, then swings eir legs behind em. Feet hook onto the beam, and Kai exhales before standing. E sways, off balance for a breathless second. Glancing down at eir T-shirt and shorts, e can't help feeling grateful e's no longer required to wear a formfitting leotard.

Kai shuffles in place, getting a feel for the narrow surface. E pulls both shoulders back. One foot extends in front of em, toes pointed. Arms out, e carefully moves forward. After all this time, the choreography's still automatic.

An arm flourish, back arched and swaying into the shape of a momentary S, Kai puts on eir "judge's smile," the expression e and Cie-Cie used to practice in the locker room before each meet. A series of small, quick steps into a tuck jump. It's not the tricky handspring e used to do, but eir pulse still flutters with pride when eir feet return to the beam.

Kai's movements are all eir own. Anyone can do a pivot, twist, or leap: a boy, a girl, or even someone like em. But after all the time e spent figuring out eir new name and pronouns, there's one thing that still stumps Kai: Why does a skill become only for girls when performed on the beam, or just for boys when executed on rings?

A split leap takes Kai to the far end of the beam in a breathless rush e hasn't felt in months. An idea forms as e moves through the rest of eir choreography. Returning to the girls' team isn't an option, but maybe Maxine will let em practice between classes. It won't be the same without eir old teammates, but Kai still approaches the end of the beam with a new lightness in each step. E cartwheels off, savoring the split second e's airborne before eir feet connect with the mat.

Behind em, someone claps.

Kai's smile widens, entirely genuine now. But it drops from eir face the moment e sees that it wasn't Maxine who was watching.

The girl doesn't seem to notice the tension rounding Kai's shoulders as e glances around the gym. Maxine shoots em a thumbs-up before disappearing into the front office.

A sea of short brown braids bounces around the girl's

cheeks as she makes her way over. "That was cool! Maxine told me there was a meet today," she says. "Did you compete?"

"No." Kai's words come fast and clipped. "I'm not a girl."

The girl tilts her head a little. "I didn't say you were."

When Kai stays quiet, the girl starts jogging in place, knees lifting high. Each of her braids seems to dance to its own choreography. "I didn't know they had a boys' team here."

Kai's chest feels tight. E can't figure out why this girl is warming up in shoes, loose pants, and a tank top instead of a leotard. "They don't."

E waits for her to ask why e was on an apparatus meant for girls, then. Cie-Cie had lots of questions after Kai told her e wasn't a girl but also didn't feel like a boy.

The girl plops onto the mat in front of Kai. "Can you jump from one to the other?"

"What?"

Legs in a wide V, she walks her hands forward. "The beams. I saw you jump on one. Think you could do the same jump but land on the beam next to it?"

"That's not—" Kai shakes eir head, but the girl can't see em with her chest pressed against the mat. "Why?"

She pushes herself back up. "Just curious. I've never seen anyone try, but it could totally work. I'm Aziza."

Work for what?

Kai shifts from foot to foot. Although e's no longer on the beam, it still feels like e's trying to find eir balance in this conversation. "Kai."

Aziza hops up, then nods toward the large mats that form the floor apparatus. She grapevines her way down one side, arms twisting, feet alternating in front of her, then behind. Kai hesitates, then joins her.

"My dad had to drop me off way before class today since he got called in to work early." Aziza switches directions when she reaches the white boundary tape at the far corner of the floor, and Kai turns with her. "Promise I wasn't spying on you."

"What class?" Kai might not train anymore, but e's positive Coach Landis and Maxine wouldn't schedule practice right after a meet.

Aziza skids to a stop, then makes big circles with her arms, rolling out her shoulders. "Parkour."

"Is that like a type of . . . dance, or something?"

"Or something." Aziza grins. "It's the art of negotiating obstacles—at least that's what our teacher, Mr. Charles, calls it."

Kai stares at her. "What does that even mean?"

"It's easier to show you. Check this out." Aziza speeds away from Kai, toward the gym wall. She swings her arms back, lifts one leg to hip height, and plants her foot on the wall. Her arms shoot up as she launches. Tucking her knees, she backflips off the wall and lands on the floor in front of it with a small rebound bounce.

"Wow." Kai's eyes go wide as Aziza sprints back to em. "Was that hard to learn?"

"It took some time." Aziza's chest rises and falls fast, then begins to slow. "I had to learn to backflip on the floor first. Then Mr. Charles had us practice launching off his hands as an assist so he could give us extra lift."

"What is your class called again? . . . Parker?"

"Park*our*. The first class just started here this summer, but a group of us have been learning for a while. We used to practice in parks and people's backyards. Still do a little. Girls and boys. Everyone." She raises her eyebrows.

Kai's stomach gives a hopeful little flutter. "And there are, like, meets you compete in as a team and stuff?"

"Nah. It's about learning tricks and stringing them together. Sometimes we'll have competitions to see who can do the coolest stuff, or share videos online. But I guess you could say we're a team. We definitely push each other."

Another flutter. "So you're seeing who can do tricks that impress people the most?"

Aziza nods. "The more creative the better. This gym's cool because we can use the equipment and set up mats to create different obstacles to get from one point to another."

"Like"—Kai pauses to imagine the possibilities—"leaping between balance beams, then swinging from the rings into the foam pit, maybe?"

"Exactly!"

Behind them, the front door opens. A man enters with a boy at his heels. The man's hair is in tight braids, just like Aziza's, but it's longer and pulled back into a thick ponytail.

"Hi, Mr. Charles. Hey, Jamal." Aziza waves at them.

"You beat us today, Queen Aziza." The man waves back. He pats Jamal's shoulder. "Go grab some mats, little man."

Kai glances at the clock as Aziza explains the reason for her early drop-off. E'll need to leave soon to be on time to pick up Lexi.

"I see you brought a friend." The man looks between them.

Aziza glances at Kai, who shakes eir head slightly. "Not for today's class," Aziza says. "But believe me, Kai's got serious skills."

"Hope to see you another week, then," Mr. Charles says. "The group could use more girls."

Kai goes completely still.

"Kai's not a girl." Aziza's voice is loud and clear.

E waits for the questions. The skeptical look. For Mr. Charles to act the same as too many people before him.

But all Mr. Charles says is, "My mistake. Nice to meet you, Kai. Come train with us sometime."

Kai heads off the floor and slips eir shoes back on. As more kids arrive, e pauses to watch them.

But e knows e can't stand there staring forever.

"See you, Kai!" Aziza calls as e heads for the door.

"Bye."

E steps outside but can't help looking back over one shoulder as kids call out to each other, then help set up mats. E closes the door and sees that someone has already taken down the competition poster. Today feels just like eir old gymnastic practices, except with one big difference.

Deep down, Kai knows what it is. If e leaves now, e'll have to wait even longer to be part of a team again.

Before e can talk emself out of it, Kai pulls out eir phone and makes a call. E lifts the phone to one ear and crosses eir fingers as tight as possible.

A FEW MINUTES LATER, KAI RUSHES BACK into the gym. The door scrapes, then sticks halfway between open and closed. E pauses, fingers curling around the door's edge. Aziza and Jamal help a couple of other kids move mats onto the floor. No one notices em at first.

"A bit more to the corner," Mr. Charles calls to Jamal. He looks over at Kai. "Welcome back."

Kai slips around the door and heads over to Mr. Charles. "I called my mom and she said I could take your class—that I can train with your team—and she'll pay when she gets here. She has to pick up my little sister first."

When Mr. Charles doesn't immediately speak, Kai rushes on. "If that's okay, I mean. I can come back next time if that works better."

Mr. Charles's eyes crinkle at the corners when he smiles. "Now's perfect."

Kai catches a double thumbs-up from Aziza and excitement tingles through eir arms and legs. Behind em, a pair of kids enter.

"Hey, Leo, Tyrese!" Aziza calls.

"Let's have y'all warm up while we wait for the stragglers," Mr. Charles says. "Kai will be joining us today."

Leo and Tyrese nod at em and begin jogging around the edges of the floor with Aziza, Jamal, and the other kids. Kai joins in as they round the first corner, running a fast circuit. Once they finish their warm-up, Mr. Charles waves them over to the edge of the floor.

"Kai"—Mr. Charles turns to em—"want to start us off?"

E swallows, eyes darting between the other kids and the floor.

"Do anything you want," Aziza says. "Anything you don't need an assist on. Mr. Charles'll help with the harder stuff later."

"Okay . . ."

Kai takes a couple of jerky steps forward before eir body remembers the timing. E reaches for the floor with both hands, feet flying over eir head and then back to the ground to complete the roundoff. Arms up by eir ears, Kai arches into a back handspring. Eir heart flutters as e punches up one more time, into a high back tuck.

The pass isn't perfect. Kai overshoots the final flip and has to jog backward out of it. Even still, a surge of joy travels from eir chest into eir limbs at being airborne again.

The gym goes quiet, and Kai waits for Mr. Charles to announce e's not right for the class, that this kind of pass is okay for gymnastics but not for parkour.

But Mr. Charles nods. "I have a feeling Kai's tumbling is going to give all y'all a run for your money."

The gym erupts in oohs, scoffs, a hoot from Jamal.

"We'll see!" one boy yells as another shakes his head, laughing.

Mr. Charles shushes them, then sends Aziza across the floor in Kai's direction. She starts with a spin on her heels, then a small leap into a somersault. Bouncing out of it light as a feather, she arches backward into what Kai thinks will be a handspring. But she lands on one hand, not both like Kai expects, and bounces in a full circle before flipping back to her feet.

Kai claps along with everyone else. "That was *awesome*," e says.

"There's a reason Mr. Charles calls me Queen." Aziza winks at Kai as a kid tumbles toward them, then another. Everyone brings something unique. Jamal's more focused on tumbling, while Tyrese's pass has a dance-like quality. Gymnastics judges would probably think their technique is sloppy, all bent knees and flexed feet. But Kai can tell from each tensed muscle that these moves require skill to look effortless.

While Mr. Charles calls out technique tips, the kids joke and challenge each other to try harder passes next time.

Parkour may be different from gymnastics, but this group still feels like a team to Kai.

As the kids run their second passes, Kai thinks about what makes em stand out. When it's only Kai and Aziza left, Aziza turns to em. "You know what you want to do next?"

There's no space left for relief or regret, just anticipation. It's the same feeling e got at the start of a routine, when eir teammates had gone quiet but e knew they were crossing their fingers, hoping e would nail every element.

E nods.

"Go for it." Aziza raises one hand, palm up, and Kai gives her a high five. Parkour may be different from gymnastics, but it also feels familiar. As Kai stares across the floor, e can't help smiling.

Shoulders back, chin high, Kai doesn't hesitate when e steps forward to tumble this time.

Come Out, Come Out Whenever You Are

BY ERIC BELL

7:53 A.M.

The morning is always the worst part, because it means I have the rest of my terrible day to look forward to.

There should be international laws against waking up before noon. Adults who force kids to do it should be shoved back in time to relive middle school, with extra acne thrown in for good measure. But the big clock in the lobby of Cliff Cliffson Middle School doesn't care. The clock, with its blinking digits, is like a call to action to brace myself for another day at the middle school proudly ranked 586th out of 802 in the entire state. (They put that on a banner draped over the football field.)

So I follow orders and I brace myself: I stand at the doors, yawn, and hope nobody looks at me.

Especially not Johnny Beacham. When Johnny Beacham looks at me, it's like my entire body is a bull's-eye, and he gets extra points for how hard he sends me flying.

"Hey, Marcus," Garrett says, approaching me with an easy smile. "Did you do your biology homework?"

"Uh, yeah," I say.

"Great," he says. "I'll be over at lunch to copy. Your handwriting's neater this time, right?"

I force my lips upward in something resembling a happy expression. "I try my best."

Well, he's not Johnny Beacham at least. Once Garrett scurries off, cockroach-with-a-donkey's-head-style, I take a deep breath and head to my locker, the one with the massive poop-colored paint stain from when they touched up the walls last week. I open it, and for a hot second, I expect Johnny Beacham to pop out like a jack-in-the-box. But he's not in here. Johnny Beacham doesn't know my combination. Maybe it's because he doesn't know any numbers above five.

"Marcus! Hey!"

Rho, another seventh grader, pops up beside me. An outrageously loud voice would normally make me jump, but because it's Rho, I'm used to it. I wouldn't call them a friend, but they're friendly enough. I give them a little smile. "Hey."

"Good to see you," they say, handing me a blank sheet of paper and a clipboard. "I'm going around and getting sign-ups for a GSA. If Principal Grant sees enough people signed up, she might make it a permanent thing." They beam at me. "GSA stands for—"

"Gender and Sexuality Alliance," I say, eyes darting around.

"Yep! It's for LGBTQ-plus kids. Allies too. The club's going to be a safe space where we can express ourselves without being judged. Do you want to sign up? I'm asking every single kid in school! You'd really love it. Everyone would."

My throat goes so dry it shrivels up. "Uh," I stammer, "I—I, uh, I don't think so."

Rho bunches their eyebrows up. "Huh? Why not?"

I shift my feet, stacking one on top of the other and then repeating it like I can build a tower of sneakers to the moon. "Uh, it's . . . it's not really my thing, I guess?"

Rho's eyebrows push together so hard a miniature black hole opens up between them, pulling me forward. "Do you have a problem with it?"

"No! No. Not at all." I grip the clipboard to stop it from shaking. Then I realize my hands are the shaky things. "I . . . I guess I'm not really, you know . . . out yet?"

Rho's mouth makes a little O shape. "I get it. No worries."

But then, like a hole in a water balloon, the words leak

out. "I mean, I, uh, I'd like to be? I guess? But people are weird and I'd hate for Johnny Beacham to find out and it'd be one thing if it was just my parents I think they suspect anyway they love throwing parties and they'd probably bake me a coming-out pie or something—" I take a deep breath.

"Marcus, it's fine," Rho says with a smile. "I won't tell anyone."

I'm sweating everywhere. The hall lights are unusually bright, like spotlights on a stage surrounded by deadly spike traps. "O-okay," I stammer. "Thanks. The last thing I want is for Johnny Beacham to be like, 'Oh, there goes Marcus, the gay kid, let's shove him inside a tree and, like, roll the tree into a beaver's nest or something.'"

"You're *gay?*" booms the largest, loudest voice imaginable.

Everything in the hall stops. Particularly my heart. I'm not sure if it'll ever start up again.

Towering over me like the world's sloppiest skyscraper is Johnny Beacham. Johnny Beacham, who emerged from his swamp just to overhear my confession. "Did you hear that, everyone? Mini Marcus is gay! No wonder no girls ever tried to date him!" He cackles this slow, gurgling cackle made of hog fat and pond scum.

My face falls to the floor. It's like Johnny Beacham is sitting on my spine, pressing it deeper and deeper into the floor. This is what I was always afraid of: his insults, even though they're ridiculous, still sting like bees with six-foot stingers. Don't get the wrong idea; there's nothing wrong with being gay. There's *everything* wrong with Johnny Beacham. He's the absolute worst person in the world. One time he made me eat his toenail clippings because he knows I'm a celiac, and he pretended to be helpful by giving me "gluten-free cuisine." He's the biggest reason I'm not out.

And now he knows.

"What's wrong, Mini Marcus?" Johnny Beacham asks, smirking like it's his full-time job. He steps closer to me, pressing me against my open locker and practically shoving me into the darkness. "Are you going to cry? Are you going to cry gay little tears?"

"Hey, that's not nice!" Rho says. But it's too late: by now everyone in the hall knows, which means by homeroom they might as well blare it over the loudspeaker, and by lunch it'll be on the CNN ticker. They'll replace the banner over the football field with one that flashes, in big neon lights, *Home of the Gay Student Whose Squishy Insides Are Permanent Target Practice*. They'll write books about me, make movies about me, take out an ad during the Super Bowl about me—and they'll all be titled *The Gay Kid Everyone Hated*.

Everyone.

I escape up the stairs with my head down and my eyes squeezed tight. I mutter a stream of nonsense to myself as I walk aimlessly through the halls: "Everything sucks. Everything is bad. I wish I never came to school today. I wish Johnny Beacham was a pineapple. I wish Johnny Beacham and Garrett and the rest of them were pineapples and I could throw them into volcanoes and run away forever because pineapples can't fight back and volcanoes are too hot for pineapples to live in anyway. I wish I never opened my awful mouth. I wish I could turn back time."

7:53 A.M.

That's what the big clock over the lobby of Cliff Cliffson Middle School says. In the lobby, not in the stairwell. Blinking neon red everywhere, waking up the student body, bracing us for the day.

I blink a few times.

Huh?

"Hey, Marcus," Garrett says, walking up to me. "Did you do your biology homework?"

I stare at him, uncomprehending.

"Hello?" he asks. "Earth to Marcus?"

"I, uh, did the homework, yeah," I say. "Didn't I already, uh, tell you that?"

"Huh?" Garrett gives me a weird look. "I'll be over at lunch to copy. Your handwriting's neater this time, right?"

"Have you seen Johnny Beacham?" I ask.

"No. Why? Is he starting up trouble again? That guy's always up to no good."

"He hasn't been spreading any . . . any rumors about me, has he?"

Garrett smirks. "Depends. Are you a creepy serial killer? Oh, wait, that's not a rumor, that's a fact. See you at lunch."

Once Garrett leaves, I scan the hall. My phone reads 7:53, so it's not like the big clock is wrong. I was at my locker and Rho asked me about the GSA and I accidentally outed myself to Johnny Beacham—my skin crawls just thinking about it—and I rambled around the stairs and now I'm back at the entrance, and it's like nobody remembers what happened in the last three minutes except me.

This is more than a little alarming. Is everyone playing a trick on me somehow? That doesn't make any sense: I was clearly at my locker for at least a minute and a half, and I don't know how they could've moved me back to the entrance without me noticing. Was I dreaming? Did I take one too many multivitamins this morning?

I stick my head inside my locker, trying not to think

too hard about déjà vu and whether week-old paint can cause hallucinations.

"Marcus! Hey!"

There's Rho, outrageously loud. They've got a sheet of paper and a clipboard. "I'm going around and getting sign-ups for a GSA. If Principal Grant sees there's enough interest in the club, she might make it a permanent thing." They beam at me. "GSA stands for—"

"Okay," I cut them off. "What's going on here? I confessed to you and now you're rubbing it in my face?"

Rho bunches their eyebrows together into a giant centipede. It's really disturbing. "What are you talking about? You never confessed anything to me."

That can't be right. "Rho, come on," I say without thinking, "I told you I was gay!"

"You're *gay*?" booms the largest, loudest voice imaginable.

Oh no. Oh no no no. Oh no no no no no—

Johnny Beacham stretches to the ceiling. Johnny Beacham breaks through the roof and eats the sun. "Hey, everybody! Mini Marcus just came out! As gay! Look at him, standing there, being gay and stuff. No wonder he's a total friendless loser!"

"I—I—that's—"

Then Johnny Beacham pulls a megaphone—literally a megaphone, it even has the initials *JB* on one side—from who even knows where and yells into it: "ATTEN-TION, EVERYONE: MINI MARCUS IS GAY. HE'S TOTALLY INTO DUDES. POINT AND LAUGH AT HIM IF YOU SEE HIM AROUND, BEING GAY. GAY GAY GAY GAY GAY." He lowers the megaphone and smirks at me. The hall is dead silent. Even Rho is speechless.

A horrible noise crawls out of my throat and I run—not walk—full-on run through the halls, escaping Johnny Beacham and escaping reality. It wasn't enough to be outed by Johnny Beacham once—it happened twice! What the heck did I do to deserve this nightmare?

And the strangest thing is, nobody else seems to remember. Not Johnny Beacham, not Rho, not Garrett. Everything replayed itself. It was like I . . .

I stop outside a bathroom, panting and sweating feverishly, and mutter, "I w-wish I could . . . turn back time."

7:53 A.M.

Lobby. Bright red clock. Bustling kids everywhere. No sign of Johnny Beacham.

Right, first things first: I need to avoid Rho altogether. If I never talk to them, I can't accidentally out myself. I take a deep breath and power walk to—

"Whoa, slow down, Marcus!" Garrett says, blocking my path. "Where's the fire?"

"Uh," I mutter. "No fire. Just busy. Busy, busy, busy." I look around in a panic for Johnny Beacham, for the Godzilla creature with fiery breath and toenail cuisine.

Garrett is unmoved by my urgency. "Not so busy you couldn't do your biology homework, right?"

"Yeah, sure. Biology. I've got to go. Business. Toenails."

Garrett shakes his head. "I'll be over at lunch, dorko. Hope your handwriting's improved."

"Sure, handwriting, got to write, got to get it right, got to—"

Oh no. There's Rho at the other end of the hall. I have to avoid them. I squeeze behind an open classroom door, throat dry again, limbs trembling again. This has to work. Once I don't out myself, I can go about my day and hope nothing else extraordinarily weird happens to me. (Maybe I should be careful about what I wish for. I don't *actually* want Johnny Beacham to turn into a pineapple. Fruit is too good for him.)

Rho keeps asking people if they want to sign up for the GSA, and nobody even gives them the time of day. I feel kind of bad. I at least *talked* to Rho. They're not thrown off, though; they keep asking everyone who walks by.

Rho's always been so comfortable with who they are, so bold and strong. They helped get a gender-neutral bathroom installed, and it's gone the whole year without anyone drawing middle fingers on the walls, which is more than I can say for the boys' bathroom.

"Hey, do you want to sign up for the GSA?" Rho booms in my direction. Oh, crap—did they see me? But no. Someone very tall is blocking the way.

"The heck is that?" Johnny Beacham asks, sneering from a doorway down the hall at Rho.

"It stands for Gender and Sexuality Alliance," Rho says. "It's for LGBTQ-plus kids. Allies too. The club's going to be a safe space where we can—"

Johnny Beacham cackles. The very sound sends high-voltage currents through my body. "Are you calling me a homo?"

Rho's eyebrows form a supereyebrow. "The club is for anyone. It's a safe space where we can—"

"Why would I go to some homo club?" Johnny Beacham laughs. "You're always stirring up stuff. Can't you be normal like everyone else?"

A deep fire blazes in my belly, but it's drowned out by the iciness in Johnny Beacham's eyes.

Rho's eyebrows furrow, burn like blacktop in the sun. Rho doesn't say anything. They don't need to. But Johnny Beacham either doesn't notice or doesn't care, and I'm not sure which is worse. He saunters off like he owns the school. Rho sighs and offers the clipboard to the next kid who walks by.

That's it. I didn't out myself. I avoided Rho, the GSA sign-up form, and Johnny Beacham. What a triumph. Now I don't have to reset time anymore. Now I can go about my business as usual. Now the world is right again.

Rho asks a group of kids to sign up, waves the empty clipboard. I wonder what it would be like to sign my name, to talk with other kids like me (there's got to be someone else, right?), to eat that terrible gluten-free coming-out pie?

I wonder what it would be like to walk out from my hiding place and say who I am, loud and clear. To not hide. To not be afraid of other people. To be . . . me.

And then I picture Johnny Beacham smashing the pie in my face.

What can I do?

Well, there's one thing I can do.

I say, "I wish I could turn back time."

7:53 A.M.

That's what the big clock over the lobby of Cliff Cliffson Middle School says. It's like a call to action to prepare for another day in the turbulent world of seventh grade at the school ranked higher than 216 other middle schools in the state. I stand at the doors, squeeze my hands into fists, and get ready to be noticed.

"Hey, Marcus," Garrett says. "Did you do your—"

"Do your own freaking homework," I say. He gasps, and I walk past him. I don't have time for Garrett. I'm on a mission. I'm looking for one kid. One kid who's been the key to this whole puzzle from the beginning. I walk past my locker, walk into the middle of the hall, walk right up to him.

"Hey, Johnny," I say.

He breaks into his fanged grin. "Mini Marcus! What's up, short guy? Still rocking that whole loser vibe, huh?"

My vision goes foggy and my legs go wobbly and my throat goes parched. I press on. "I have—I have something to tell you."

"Huh? Listen, dude, it's cool that you still wet the bed and your pee is brown from all those almonds you eat and you've got an extra toe growing out of your armpit and all, but—"

"I'm gay."

Johnny Beacham stares at me.

I stare back. "I mean, you know, maybe, sure," I say. "Probably. Yeah. Probably."

Then he cracks up. "Hey, everyone, did you hear

that? Mini Marcus is gay! He just confessed that he's totally into dudes. What a freaking loser!"

His words hurt. They pelt me with spears, tear holes in my skin. But he'd make fun of me no matter what, so I might as well try to be happy. True to myself. I look around the hall for the first time in all these todays, and most people don't even care. A few kids point and stare. A few look at me with smiles.

"Marcus! Hey!" Rho comes over, paper and clipboard bouncing around. "That was amazing, wow! I'm so proud of you."

I blush. "Thanks. Let me guess: Sign-ups for a GSA?"

"Yep! Are you interested?"

I picture my name on the paper. I hear myself laughing and joking in a safe space. I can almost taste that gluten-free pie with just the right amount of whipped cream. But I also know it's been, like, literally fifteen seconds since I came out (well, fifteen seconds in this timeline at least). Sometimes, before you take the leap, you need to get used to what the ground looks like first.

"Not yet," I say. "Maybe someday."

Rho's eyebrows knit into a heart. "We'll be here whenever you are." They offer the clipboard to someone else.

My whole body trembles. My nerves have been

shocked, my heart's been spiked, my brain's been fried. In spite of all this, I feel . . . I feel . . . I feel—

"I don't get it," Johnny Beacham says, studying me. The hall is still packed, but for this moment, it's just us.

"No," I say. "You don't. I hope someday you do."

"Just wait, Mini Marcus," he sneers. "You can't get rid of me. Turn around, and I'll be there, chasing you around the football field or shoving toenails down your throat. I'll always be here."

I stare up at Johnny Beacham. "I know. But *I'll* always be here too. I love myself, and that's enough to fight people like you."

Johnny Beacham scrunches up his face. "That's the gayest thing I've ever heard."

I take a deep breath and smile. "Yeah. It is."

Devoyn's Pod

BY MARIAMA J. LOCKINGTON

FACT: A group of whales is called a pod. Pods can consist of a bunch of whales that are biologically connected, but pods can also form through friendships developed by two or more whales.

ME, ELLA, AND MARCEL HAVE BEEN FRIENDS since first grade. Since our moms walked us the few blocks over from Fort Greene Park to PS 20, kissed us on our big-little heads, and shoved us away. We were some big-little heads full of questions, thinking we were all grown up not having to be on one of those preschool leash lines anymore. Big-little heads who all ended up in Ms. Gupta's first-grade class, our cubbies next to one another's because our last names are alphabetical: Devoyn Parker (that's me), Ella Quintanilla, and Marcel Randolph. Now we're not so little—about to be eighth graders—but our heads are still big, full of dreams, questions, and ideas. Today is the first day of summer break, and that means none of us have anywhere to be but together. On top of that, it's Saturday and as sunny as a sunny-side-up egg. I can't wait to get outside.

I'm so ready I'm eating my cereal standing at the kitchen counter. Nana Billie sits flipping through her newspaper while hot black coffee steams from her favorite Reclaiming My Time mug.

"Why don't you sit down, Devy?" she says, not looking up from what she's reading. "Your friends will wait."

Nana Billie is my mom's mom and the only person I let call me Devy. I prefer Dev for short. Mom and I have been living with her ever since I can remember on the garden level and first level of her brownstone off the park. Nana Billie rents out the other two floors to bougie white people, who seem to be everywhere nowadays.

"Back in my prime time," Nana Billie likes to tell me on wash days, when we sit and watch Spike Lee movies as she runs her hands through my curls, "Fort Greene was full of us: Black entrepreneurs, artists, and writers like me. Your mom wasn't but two years old when Spike Lee moved his 40 Acres and a Mule studio into that three-story firehouse on DeKalb. By the time you came along in 2008, he was forced out of that building, had to move his studio to Elliott Place, where it is now."

Even I can tell how things have changed in the hood, how nowadays the DeKalb Avenue side of the park is full of faces that don't look like mine, or El's, or Marcel's. At least the Myrtle Avenue side is still pretty Black. This is the side me, El, and Marcel post up at. See, even though Marcel is obsessed with running track and basketball, and El wants to be a writer and I'm going to be a marine biologist one day, the park is the glue that holds us together. I call us a pod because to this day that's what we are: not super social with other kids, but that's because we're super-tight friends. We don't need anybody else swimming with us in this city; that's how you get lost in the crowd. Having two best friends is all I need. Facts. Two best friends—and Nana Billie and Mom, of course.

Mom comes in just as I am slurping the milk from my cereal bowl. She's wearing her royal-purple uniform and rolling her carry-on behind her. Mom loves the sky the way I love the water, and her job as a flight attendant keeps her gone almost every week.

"Devoyn Shiree Parker. Sit at the table and eat like a lady. You know better."

"I'm finished. I'm supposed to meet El and Marcel in fifteen."

Mom walks over to me and starts to wind my twists up into a thick bun.

"Ow! That's too tight."

"I'm just trying to get them off your beautiful face."

"I like wearing them down."

"Why don't you throw on a sundress? It's so nice out."

I scrunch my face. I like what I'm wearing: jean shorts, my faded red high-top Chucks, and a soft tie-dyed T-shirt with a bunch of orca whales swimming around planet Earth.

"I'm good," I say.

"Fine. Give me some love, then." Mom gives up and lets go of my hair. "I'll be back early Monday morning so I can send you off to marine biology camp."

I'll believe it when I see it. When it comes to getting up early on one of her days off, Mom doesn't have a great track record.

"Okay. Fly safe," I say, giving her a quick kiss, and then, to Nana Billie, "I'll be back around two."

Before either of them can remember anything else they need me to do, I'm out the door.

FACT: An octopus has three hearts: one pumps blood to the body, and the other two pump blood to the gills. All three help the creature stay alive and active.

WHEN I GET TO OUR SPOT ON THE MYRTLE

side of the park, neither El nor Marcel is there yet, but that's okay. I'm the most on time in our pod. I sit up against a tree and look out over the park. It's only nine-thirty, but it's a whole scene—people sitting on blankets, the jungle gym overflowing with small kids and toddlers, buff dudes doing pull-ups on the training bars, old heads sitting out on their folding chairs playing checkers, folks setting up their Saturday family BBQs and playing loud R & B jams on portable speakers. The park is really just a microcosm of the larger city. My little part of New York. The only home I've ever known. When I look at the park like this, I feel like I'm in my natural habitat. It's when I think about how much more of the city is out there that I start to feel small and overwhelmed.

"Boo!" El whispers in my ear a few moments later. Her soft, shoulder-length black hair swings against my cheek, and I inhale the smell of it. El always smells like lemons and fresh-air Febreze. She's wearing her typical outfit: skinny jeans with black-and-white Air Jordans, a white T-shirt, and lots of beaded and woven bracelets. Her dimples wink at me when she smiles, and a school of sailfish flutters in my chest.

"Heyo," Marcel says, sitting down next to me on the ground as he laces up his shoes. Marcel is tall and lanky, with an impressive Afro that gleams in the sunlight. Kids at school tease him by calling him Starvin' Marcel, but El and I know that he can eat four times the food we can in one sitting. Plus, we know that the way he's built means Marcel runs like a shooting star.

"Hey, nerds," I say, "you're late."

"My bad," El says, plopping down next to me and pulling out her story book. "Had to look after Luna this morning. Mom worked a late shift and needed to sleep in." El takes care of her two-year-old sister a lot. I nod and give her a fist bump.

"I'm just late." Marcel laughs. "You know me. Got out of bed like fifteen minutes ago. Ain't even had break-fast yet."

"Here," I say, pulling a granola bar out of my bag. "I got you."

Marcel eats the granola bar in two quick bites, and then El hands him her water bottle without saying any-thing. He grins and grabs it, takes a huge swig, and then stands up.

"All right, all right. I'm feeling good. Feeling fine. Ready to make this day mine!"

El and I roll our eyes, then yell: "Ready, set, GO!"

Marcel takes off running up and down the monument steps for his daily workout. I love how his energy feeds ours, like we all share the same heartbeat, the same blood, the electricity of his movement waking us up.

As Marcel runs, El starts reading me one of her latest short stories, and I lie with my head in her lap. It's a ghost story about a girl who visits an abandoned house and can't find her way out of it and then slowly becomes the house. It's one of El's masterpieces, and I get so lost in the story that I hardly notice when she stops reading and begins to gawk over her shoulder at something.

I sit up and see that she is watching Marcel. Marcel has taken off his tank top at the top of the stairs and is using it to wipe sweat from his brow.

"Gross," I say, even though I also notice how broad his shoulders have gotten, how all the baby fat from his face has faded away. But El is drooling, mouth open, and I'm not sure she can even hear me. I want her to look at me again.

"Earth to El," I say, waving a hand in her face.

El snaps her head back around and smiles. "Yeah. Sweat is mad gross."

"So," I say, wanting El to start reading her story again, "what happens next?"

El closes her notebook and shrugs. "Don't know yet. That's as far as I got."

"Well, it's really good. Maybe Ms. Wells will help you with it when you start Story Bootcamp next week." Ms. Wells teaches sixth-grade English at our school, but during the summer she runs a middle school creative writing camp for all grades. El has been a part of the camp for the last two summers.

"She's not going to story camp." Marcel is back. He plops down next to me, and I can feel the heat radiating off his body. He smells like grass and wind.

"Yeah, she is," I say, pushing him on his arm.

"No. I'm, uh . . . ," El begins. "I'm going to Y Camp . . . with Marcel."

"Since when?" All the muscles in my neck and shoulders tighten, and I make my eyes all squinty, like an octopus's.

"Since I asked my mom to sign me up for it. Plus, Marcel made it sound all fun last summer."

"Yeah, but Marcel likes playing sports and doing team activities. You hate all that."

"Well, maybe I want to try something new this summer. And maybe it will help me write some other kind of story, kind of like research or something for a sports-themed mystery."

"That doesn't even make sense," I say, but then again, El could probably make any kind of story good.

Marcel is quiet. Normally, he and I'd be teasing El about her lack of athletic ability.

"So that means you two will be together most of the summer? And I'll be by myself. . . ." This hasn't been an issue before. Before, we all went to different camps and then convened in the afternoons or on weekends to catch up and hang out. Suddenly it doesn't feel like our heartbeats are in sync at all.

"Yeah, but we know how much you love that fish camp you go to," Marcel says. "And El and I probably won't even be in the same group at Y Camp. They break us up into like three different groups."

"You don't think we'll be in the same group?" El says, her eyes widening as she looks at Marcel. "What if I want to be in the same group?"

At the same time, I say, "It's at the aquarium, Marcel. It's not a fish camp."

It's actually a marine biology camp. I've gone the last two years, but this year, since I'm going to be an eighth grader and one of the oldest kids there, I get to kind of help out and teach the younger kids. I'm pretty excited about it, but this new information about El and Marcel being together makes me feel, well, weird.

Marcel clears his throat. "I mean, yeah, I want to be in the same group as you too, El, but we'll have to see."

I watch El's face turn into a rain cloud. It's time to change the subject. Things are starting to feel not like a typical pod Saturday.

"Let's go get Icee pops?" I say, standing up and wiping the grass off my shorts. "Since we all start camp on

Monday, might as well make the best of our day together, right?"

Technically, we're not supposed to leave the park when we hang out, even though we're all thirteen. Those are the boundaries our moms gave us: the park and a couple of the surrounding bodegas, then we better bring our butts right on home. But the best Icee pops are a few blocks away, and every now and then, we break our moms' rules. We come right back to the park, of course, because none of us want to get grounded.

"Yes!" Marcel says.

"Okay," El says, perking up.

"Race you there!" I yell, running fast down the hill, knowing I have no chance against Marcel unless I get a head start. Behind me, I feel the two of them scrambling to their feet to follow. I try to ignore the upset feeling in my gut as I run, my insides tangled like a net full of plastic trash. *Everything is going to be great,* I say to myself. *Just like it always is. Just the three of us.*

FACT: Orca grandmas help raise their grandkids till they're like nine years old.

MOM IS OUT OF TOWN AGAIN THE NEXT

weekend, so on Saturday, Nana Billie and I have the house to ourselves. Friday night, I texted the pod to make sure we were meeting in the park at the normal time, but El and Marcel never responded. Normally, after our first week apart from one another, we have lots to catch up on.

You up? I text now. *R we meeting today?*

"No phone at the table," Nana Billie says from behind her coffee mug.

"I'm just trying to figure out where El and Marcel are."

"Well, then get up from the table."

I look down at my phone. Nothing. I slip it into my pocket and focus on breakfast. Nana Billie got us bagels this morning. I grab a sesame bagel and pop it in the toaster. When the toaster dings, I slather half the bagel with plain cream cheese and the other with peanut butter. Both combos are my favorite; I can never choose just one.

"So, how was camp this week?" Nana Billie asks, putting down her mug and focusing her speckled brown eyes on me, her Afro a perfectly even halo of silver curls framing her face.

I'm midbite, and I know better than to talk with my mouth full, so I nod and chew, which gives me some time to think about how I want to answer that: truthfully or easily.

I decide on the latter. "Did you know that starfish eat inside out? Instead of putting food into their stomachs, their stomachs come OUT OF THEIR MOUTHS to eat the food and then go back into their body when they are done digesting it. Also, they're not even fish. They're more related to sea urchins. We got to help . . ." I go on and on. Fact after fact, until I'm out of breath.

"So, it sounds like you're enjoying learning. I'm glad," Nana Billie says slowly. "Any new friends?"

I take another bite. A big one. I shake my head. When I'm done chewing, I say, "No. But that's okay."

Nana Billie leaves it at that, for now. But I can sense we're not done talking about this. Making friends outside of the pod has always been hard for me.

My phone buzzes in my pocket. I jump up and stand by the sink so I can check the text without Nana Billie getting mad.

EL: Sry, Dev. Me and Marcel went to hang at the
    basketball courts with some of his Y friends
    last night.

What other friends? Why didn't they ask me to come?

ME: Ok. What r u up to now? Want to meet at the
    spot?
EL: . . .

ME: ???

EL: Marcel and I were thinking about going to the Soul
    Sound party instead. Both our families will be there.
    Can you come too?

ME: That old-people dance party in the park?

MARCEL: LOL, Dev. Yes. That one. We can make fun
    of everyone's moves. It will be fun.

EL: Plus, we can sneak away to our spot if it gets too
    boring.

ME: Ok. What time? Have to ask Nana B.

EL: 4 pm. Top of the steps.

I look at my watch. It's not even ten a.m. *What am I
supposed to do all day?*

ME: Ok. See u there.

MARCEL: 💃

EL: 😍 🙂

ME: 🦄 ✊🏾

HOURS LATER, NANA BILLIE AND I MAKE

our way over to the park, taking our time to climb the
hilly path up to the monument, where we can already

hear the DJ spinning beats. When we finally get to the top, I scan the crowd for El and Marcel.

"I'll be right here, Devy," Nana Billie calls out, plopping herself down on a nearby bench. "You know I love to watch people. I sure do like to see the folks get free on that dance floor. Go on and find your friends, and then come find me later."

I kiss Nana Billie on the cheek and push past the DJ booth toward the center of the crowd. The crowd is really a true mix of Black, white, and brown, and for once folks seem to be smiling, dancing, and getting along, unconcerned with what side of the park they are on. The DJ is spinning house music, so there's a good beat, but the way people dance is all up to what their bodies are telling them. I skirt the perimeter of the crowd until I make it to the monument side. I don't see my friends, so I pull out my phone and text.

ME: Here. Where u at?

I circle the crowd a few more times, but still no El and Marcel. I spot Mrs. Quintanilla and Mrs. Randolph, El's and Marcel's moms, under a nearby tree.

"Have you seen El and Marcel?" I ask.

"Dev, you're getting so tall!" Mrs. Quintanilla says. "I hardly recognized you."

"I guess so," I say, hunching my shoulders.

"I think they're on the dance floor," Mrs. Quintanilla

says, waving her hand toward the middle of the thick crowd. "Go on, they're waiting for you."

I say a quick thanks and then face the dance floor. I take a deep breath and plunge into it. I get about two layers of dancing bodies in before I see them. I spot Marcel's Afro first, then El's black bob bouncing up and down. I raise my hand to yell at them but stop in my tracks. They are dancing, but not just dancing in a silly circle like we normally all do. *They're dancing together.* The net full of trash in my gut slams against the wall of my stomach. I watch as El faces Marcel and throws her arms around his shoulders, and as Marcel puts his hands on El's hips. They kind of dip and move their hips and OMG are they *grinding?* El is giggling and Marcel looks mad sweaty and focused on her face, and then, as though this is one of those gross romantic comedies my mom loves, Marcel leans down and kisses El *on the mouth.*

"WHAT ARE YOU GUYS DOING?" I yell just as the song fades out.

El and Marcel pull away from each other quick, but both of them have stupid grins on their faces.

"Hi, Dev!" El says, breathless.

"What's up?" Marcel adds.

I cross my arms and tap my foot. I shrug and motion my hands toward the both of them like, *I dunno, what is up?* I feel super dizzy.

"Look," El starts, gesturing for the two of us to join her on the outskirts of the crowd.

I push ahead of Marcel to get to her first.

"Don't be mad, Dev," El starts. Marcel is shuffling his feet and looking at the ground.

"We wanted to tell you today," she continues.

"Tell me what, exactly? And what happened to you yesterday? I texted you both!"

"Yeah," Marcel pipes up. "We were hanging out—"

"I know, you were hanging out with your 'other friends,' but we always check in on Fridays. So, what, now you're kissing on each other to, like, fit in or something?"

Now it's El's turn to look down at her shoes. "We're not pretending," she says softly.

"You're not?"

"No," Marcel says. "El's my girlfriend. Deadass."

"We're dating."

My mouth goes dry and I have to swallow a few times. I pull absentmindedly on a few of my twists, and the sharp throb of my scalp is evidence that this is in fact real life. I am not dreaming. My body goes numb as I scan the earnest, bashful faces of my friends, my pod.

"Oh" is all I manage, and the three of us just stand there.

"But"—Marcel coughs—"we're still friends too."

"Friends who kiss," I say. "So, for how long has this been happening?"

"A week," El says.

"I mean, I been liking El for a long time," Marcel says, back to shuffling his feet. "But we made it official at Y Camp this week."

He did? Why didn't he tell me? So, that's why they were being so weird last week. I feel a crack in my chest, like the oceanic mantle shifting, and then a rush of anger. Pods are supposed to stick together, to be loyal no matter what. Pods are not supposed to have secrets and pair off.

"Come on, Dev. It's no big deal. We're still the same El and Marcel. We just, you know, are also dating." El says this as we walk over to the top steps of the monument. And then, as if nothing major is happening, she starts to do the robot dance to the song that's playing. "We're still tight, Dev. We still got jokes. Look, look how good I can dance this old dance."

I want to laugh and join El, because El is always good at making me smile. In fact, most days when I wake up, the first thing I think about is her smile, and how when I get close to her, my skin feels like it's glowing, like I'm bioluminescent. But it's not the same today. Marcel starts to do his version of an old dance, walking around like he's rolling around an invisible shopping cart and grabbing things off an imaginary shelf to dump in the cart. This is where I would normally jump in with a really bad, off-beat version of the running man, but instead I just watch the two of them dancing together. They are laughing and staring into each other's eyes all gooey-like. All of El's warmth is turned toward Marcel, and Marcel is soaking her energy up like it's the sun.

"I don't feel good," I say, close to tears. "I gotta go find Nana Billie. See you later." And before either of them can convince me to stay, I run into the middle of the dance floor and then bust out the other side. When I look behind me, it's just a mess of folks dipping and twirling and enjoying getting free on a Saturday afternoon. I wish I was getting free, but I just feel alone.

FACT: Sea otters can live their whole lives without leaving the water. To keep from drifting apart from their pods when they sleep, they will hold paws as they slumber.

WHEN NANA BILLIE AND I GET HOME, I GO

right to my room.

"Dinner will be in an hour," she says after me.

I close the door and throw myself down on my bed. Something is bubbling up inside. All at once my room is a whirlpool and I start to swirl away from everything I thought was true. I think about how Marcel's hands were on El's waist on the dance floor, how she didn't seem to mind him being all up in her space. El never lets me that close, even when I lay my head in her lap. Once, last summer, I asked her if she would twirl my twists with her fingers while she read. I like that feeling of someone tugging soft on my scalp, sending light tickles down my neck. But El just laughed, popped her gum, and said, "Quit playing, Dev. I'm not going to be all up in your hair." So I left it at that, but now my scalp is itching with envy thinking about how Marcel said, "I been liking El for a long time," and how El's whole face bloomed with soft pinks.

Do I also like El? The thought is as small as a dwarf pygmy goby, so small at first, I hardly recognize it. But then it gets louder until it roars in my chest like a great white. *What does she even see in Marcel's skinny self?*

But deep down, I know what it is. I've seen it too.

One rainy day this spring, it was just me and Marcel after school. El had to go home and take care of Luna, but Marcel and I didn't feel like being cooped up inside yet. It had rained all day, so the court was damp and full of little bits of trees that had fallen in the wind. Besides a couple of high schoolers on the other end, it was just the two of us.

"Let's play horse," Marcel said, dribbling the ball toward me, then ducking around me and shooting into the hoop.

"I think we know who's gonna win."

"Me?"

"Uh, no. Obviously me."

I grabbed the ball as it rebounded and then made my own shot. I'm not great at basketball, but I can shoot. We got through two games (we each won a game) before we quit. I don't remember the last time the two of us had that much fun without El.

"Wanna get a snack?" Marcel asked.

"I don't have any money," I said.

"I got you." Marcel smiled and put his arm around my shoulders.

He did this all the time, but normally he'd throw one arm around El and one arm around me, and we'd all try to walk the block in unison, only breaking apart to let someone else on the sidewalk go past.

But with just the two of us it felt different. Marcel was walking and talking like it was nothing, but I was thinking about the weight of his arm on my shoulder, surprised by all his new muscles. I could smell his sweat, and his scent was new, like a grown-up man, but also like the Marcel I'd known since first grade.

"Yo, what are you doing, Dev! Back up, fam."

I hadn't meant to be so obvious about it, but without thinking, I'd leaned my head into Marcel's armpit and inhaled the rainy, curious smell of him. I was so embarrassed I punched his arm lightly and said, "Calm down, I'm just messing with you. You smell like a funky cheese factory."

"I thought you were about to lick my armpit or something."

"Ew. Why would I do that? Stop playing."

"You're a weird one, Dev."

"So?"

"I just mean there's no one like you."

I smiled then. And when he smiled back, I realized how handsome he was.

I didn't want to kiss Marcel, but I understood why someone would. I just didn't think it would be El.

In my room now, a hot, hot rage seeps up, and I throw my face into my pillow and scream. My head aches and all I want is for things to go back to the way they were before: uncomplicated. The three of us with our arms thrown around one another, floating through the city, never letting go.

Nana peeks her head in when I don't come out for dinner.

"You okay, baby?" she asks, coming over to my bed and rubbing my back in circles. "What's wrong?"

I sit up and let her hug me tight. I'll never be too old for Nana Billie's hugs.

After a long while, I ask, "Why do people have to date and fall in love?"

Nana Billie laughs, but not at me. She laughs like she's thinking about someone from her past. "Oh, Devy, I'm guessing this has to do with Ella and Marcel?"

I nod. "It's gross."

Nana Billie laughs again. "Love is a wonderful thing, Devy. But I know it can be confusing and scary sometimes, and maybe it feels easier to believe you don't want it. But you'll find your person, Devy. I know you will. When you're ready, of course. And that person, they'll make you feel all gross and gooey too."

"What if I don't find that person?"

"You will. And whoever they are, they'll be lucky to have you. Now dry your face and come eat this spaghetti with me, okay? And ease up on those friends of yours. I know they still need you."

"Okay."

What I don't ask her is the question under the question: *What if the person I love doesn't love me back in the way I want them to?*

FACT: Many species of sea turtles are endangered. Major threats to their existence include getting struck by ships or tangled in fishing nets.

A LOT OF PEOPLE STILL THINK THAT BLACK

people can't swim, but that's a stereotype. Nana Billie set it straight for me. It's not that Black people don't know how to swim, don't like to, or don't want to learn; it's because for a long time, people like us weren't allowed to use public pools or public beaches. For a long time, we were kept out, and if we did dare to dip our bodies into the water, the whole pool would be shut down so they could drain and clean the pool of our "dirty."

"I'm so glad you love the water," Nana Billie said to me the first time she came to one of my meets in fifth grade. "Took me a long time to get comfortable even soaking my legs in a pool. When I was your age, we'd just crack open the fire hydrant and run through it. Pools weren't for us."

I think about this every time I dive into the water at the Y. I can't imagine being afraid of the water and swimming like that. When I swim, I feel free. All the parts of me that don't make sense come together. So, the next day, the Sunday after the Soul Sound party, that's what I do. While Nana Billie takes her Zumba class, I head right to the pool. Mr. Jake is the lifeguard on duty, and I like Mr. Jake. He knows me because he was the one who administered the swim test that proved I was skilled enough to swim without a parent or guardian poolside.

"Hey there, Miss Dev. What are we swimming today? Freestyle or breaststroke?"

"Definitely freestyle," I say as I adjust my goggles over my swim cap.

"Excellent, that's your best stroke. Enjoy. I'll flag you down when I see your grandma come in."

I smile. Mr. Jake knows me well enough to know I'd keep swimming all day if Nana Billie didn't come to collect me.

"Hey," Mr. Jake calls, "when are you bringing that friend of yours Emma back to swim?"

My shoulders get tight. Ella. He's talking about El.

"She seemed like a good swim buddy. I don't see you with too many other young people."

"She's around" is all I say, and then I jump into the pool and push off from the side. I don't come up for air until I am almost a quarter of the way down the lap lane. When I do surface, I swim as hard and as fast as I can away from Mr. Jake's question and the image of El and Marcel kissing. I get all tangled in the memory. So tangled that before I know it, Mr. Jake is tapping me on the head to let me know Nana Billie is waiting. I stand up and shake my head to get the water out of my ears, and the sounds of the world come rushing back in. I cough a little, out of breath.

"You okay, Miss Dev?" Mr. Jake asks, looking concerned. "Seemed like you were trying to get away from something out there."

I shrug, and because I'm feeling brave, I say, "I'm a Black girl in America, Mr. Jake. Everything's out to get me."

Mr. Jake doesn't know what to say to that, so I shake my hair out of my swim cap and walk away to hit the showers.

FACT: Humpback whales communicate through songs: howls, wails, and cries that are produced when the whales push air around their head and use the piece of fat that sits on their jaw to amplify the sound.

EL AND I KISSED ONCE TOO. WELL, AT LEAST

that's what it was to me. Not long after playing horse with Marcel, I convinced El to come swimming with me at the Y one Saturday.

"Fine," she'd said over the phone, "but I'm not doing any laps. I'm not a dolphin or an orca or any of those other sea beasts you love. I like to float and do headstands. I'm more like a happy hippo."

"Fine. No laps," I said. "But you should know, hippos are pretty deadly."

When we arrived at the pool, I tried not to peek at El

pulling on her swimsuit in the locker room, but it was hard not to. El has never been shy about her body a day in her life, and she's never been taller than a boy or had to deal with having a flat chest. I put on my swimsuit— a navy-blue one-piece with thick straps—while El shimmied into her black tankini.

"Hey!" she said. "What am I?" She put her arms down by her side and started to wobble back and forth.

"Oh, hey there, Happy Feet!" I joked in a baby voice. "Hey there, lil' penguin."

El snorted and grabbed her towel. "Let's go!"

When we got to the pool, free swim had just started. I put on my swim cap and goggles, but El jumped right in, and when she came up for air, her hair was all shiny and black, matted against her face. It was so black and shiny it looked like licorice.

"What are you waiting for? Get in!"

"You're so bossy!" I yelled.

"And don't you forget it!" she yelled back.

As promised, I didn't make El swim laps or even swim any myself. Instead, we floated on our backs, we splashed around, we tried to see who could do a handstand the longest while holding our breath underwater.

"Want to hear an underwater story?" El said after a while.

"A what?"

"You know, like how whales communicate or whatever. I'll tell a story underwater and you try to figure out what I'm saying."

I giggled. "Sounds impossible. Whale song is highly sophisticated—"

But before I could launch into a full fact-bomb rant, El took a deep breath and went under. I pulled on my goggles and did the same.

Underwater, El began to gargle and move her hands around, speaking in muted, echoey tones. Big bubbles burst from her mouth and nose, and it was all really cute and comical.

When we came back up, she said, "So! What story was I telling?"

"I have no idea."

"Come on, Dev. Yes, you do."

"I don't. Give me another clue."

El bit her lip, and I could tell she was tapping her foot impatiently under the water. "Fine."

Then she took another deep breath and went under again. I followed and watched as El moved her arms as if she was drinking something, seeming to sob and cry, and then she came toward me and put her mouth on mine, blowing small, soft bubbles into my mouth, before stopping movement and then lying on her back until she floated to the surface.

I swam up after her, and when I got above water, she was still floating on her back, eyes closed and arms crossed.

"*Romeo and Juliet?*" I asked.

"BINGO!" she yelled, standing up and wiping the hair out of her eyes. "You got it."

I grinned and then touched my lips. El was already thinking through the next underwater story to tell me, but I was remembering her mouth filling my mouth with bubbles. Her lips on my lips, like a song. How underwater, we were more than girls, more than just friends, but two beautiful creatures, exchanging breath in the deep water.

FACT: Female gray reef sharks give birth to a litter of three to six shark pups. Once born, the pups live on their own and don't need their mom to survive.

AFTER WE EAT OUR SUNDAY-NIGHT PIZZA and watch *Crooklyn*, Nana Billie and I head to bed. I check my phone and see that both El and Marcel have texted about meeting at the park after camp tomorrow. I don't answer. I put on my whale song mix and watch the streetlights flicker around my room, and for a little while I forget everything. I float around in a deep blue darkness.

The next morning, I'm up and dressed by seven, and Nana Billie sets a plate of eggs and bacon on the table for me. The door to Mom's room is shut tight, and I don't hear her stirring.

"Let her sleep," Nana Billie says. "She got in late last night."

I nod. Nana Billie must catch my long look toward Mom's room because she hands me my lunch and says, "Devy, you know she won't get up before noon. She'll see you later, okay?"

I scrunch up my face and cross my arms like a toddler. I know I should be a big girl about this, but I feel all newborn and clingy.

"Devy?" Nana Billie continues.

"What?"

"Your mom loves you, and so do I, but us Parker women, we're not always good at playing by the rules, okay? We're different. Independent. We love hard, but sometimes we follow our own paths no matter what the world is telling us to do. You'll see. I can tell you're on your own path too. Now get your butt up and off to camp. We didn't pay all that money so you could sit here and mope."

Nana Billie kisses my head, and I know the conversation is over. Nana Billie always tells the truth, but even when it is harsh, it's gentle.

FACT: Starfish contain most of their vital organs in their arms. Sometimes, over the course of a year, they can regenerate a whole new starfish from a severed arm.

WHEN I AM AT CAMP, I LOSE MYSELF IN THE

creatures. I can't have my phone on me, so I don't have to worry about what I'm going to text back to El and Marcel. In the morning, I help run a starfish petting zoo for the kindergartners, and it's fun watching their little hands squirm as they hold the stars and let them slide around on their palms. In the afternoon, I help them build their own coral reef out of clay, cardboard, and paint. By two p.m., I'm feeling a little more like myself.

On my way home, I check my phone, and sure enough, El has texted.

EL: Dev. Don't be this way. We still love you.

MARCEL: For sure. Pod life forever. Are you coming to the park today?

I shake my head. I'm not ready.

I text back: Maybe tomorrow, I'm too 😴

WHEN I GET HOME, I FIND A POST-IT WITH

Mom's handwriting on my bedroom door. It reads: *Got*

an extra shift, going to Portugal! See you this weekend. Love, Mom.

I crumple the note and flop onto my bed to stare at the ceiling.

"I thought I heard you come in. How was camp today?" Nana Billie says, cracking open my door.

"It was fine."

"Are you headed to the park to see those friends of yours?"

"Not likely," I say.

"What's going on, Devy? This isn't like you."

"What's the point? They'll probably just be all over one another, act like I'm not even there."

"I see," Nana Billie says. "I know this is a new dynamic for your group, but all friend groups go through growing pains. And, like I said, the fact that they've been texting you and reaching out means they still need you."

"Sure," I say. "But everything is all confusing now. And what if nobody ever wants to date me?"

Nana doesn't say anything, just sits down on the bed and holds my feet in her lap.

"Devy, everybody loves you. You have to love yourself too."

"Will you love me even if I end up with someone who's more like El than Marcel?"

Nana Billie looks at me long, her expression full of

softness. "Yes. I've known you your whole life, Devy. You are a unique, intelligent, out-of-the-box kind of girl. Just like me, and just like your mom. I don't care who you end up with. Long as they treat you well."

I let a few tears fall. I've been holding that in forever, it seems.

"Listen," Nana says, looking at her watch, "I have an idea. Get your bathing suit on."

"I don't feel like the pool," I say.

"Well, we're not going to the pool. It's only three-thirty. If we go now, we can catch a nice sunset."

"Go where?"

"You'll see. Bring a towel too. I'll get some food packed up."

An hour and a half later, we're at the beach. But not Coney Island, where I've been a thousand times. "I think you're old enough to know about this place, Devy," Nana Billie says as we take off our sandals and start walking toward the water.

We are at Riis Park Beach in Queens, which Nana Billie tells me is "the people's beach."

"What people?" I ask.

"Well, people like us."

"Black people?"

"Yes. And people who love who they want to love."

Nana Billie says this last part just as she takes off her long floral cover-up and spreads out on her towel. She's wearing a polka-dot black-and-white one-piece and a big straw hat.

"You mean . . . gay people?"

"Yes. Gay, bisexual, lesbian—queer, I think, is the word some of the young folks like. In my time, that word was a slur, but now I hear it's been reclaimed."

I don't know what to say. I look around the part of the beach we're on, and at first I just see families with kids. But I realize I'm not seeing everything. Two women splash into the water ahead of us, and one dips the other as if they are dancing. Then they kiss and dive under the waves.

"This part of the beach requires clothing," Nana says. "But over there, all the way down there, you don't even have to wear a bathing suit if you don't want to."

"You mean it's a *nude* beach?" I feel my face go hot.

"I think so," Nana Billie says. "I don't need to be doing all that, but I'm glad it's there for those who do."

"Wow!" is all I can manage.

"You can go explore a little if you want to, just don't go in the water unless you're over here in front of me, and stay on the path if you go down to that end. And take your phone!"

I nod. I'm warm on the sand next to Nana Billie. I'm a little scared to leave her side. I can't believe she brought me to a gay beach. But then again, Nana Billie said it best: *Parker women follow their own paths.* Someday I'm going to ask Nana Billie about who she thought of when I asked her that question about love.

Nana Billie starts to read a book. I get up to use the bathroom, and then I stroll down the beach on the paved path. I walk away from the sounds of toddlers running screaming into the water, toward the sound of music, of laughter, of more brown and Black bodies glistening in the heat. It takes me a moment to realize that I'm seeing so much glistening skin because folks on this part of the beach are topless—all over the sand, people are sitting in little pods, eating strawberries, drinking canned beverages from coolers, standing and dancing on blankets. I see two folks napping in each other's arms under a hot-pink umbrella. I see a person with scars like wings on their chest pull off their shirt and go chasing after their friends into the waves. I see so many kinds of ways to be, all strewn in front of me.

I watch this beach full of colorful clusters—arms and legs splayed out in various configurations—and all at once I know what I need to do. I pull out my phone and text: *We're regenerating.*

El responds right away, and my stomach flips just knowing she's still there for me:

EL: Hi! ☺ We miss you. We're at the park. What's that mean?

MARCEL: Say what now?

I try to quiet the pounding in my chest. Even if I don't understand all the parts that make me *me* yet, and even though it hurts that El isn't *my* person, at least I know I'm not alone. At least I have this beach, my friends, and Nana Billie.

ME: I think maybe we're not a pod anymore. I think we might be more like a constellation of starfish — like we're regrowing ourselves into something new. I'm not mad. I just have some stuff I need to tell you both . . . about me. Meet you at the park tomorrow?

EL: Yes! We have so much to tell you too. Also, starfish are extra cute, cuter than whales, TBH. ⭐

MARCEL: Ur always so deep with fact bombs, Dev. I'll for sure be there.

ME: Tomorrow, 3 pm sharp. Our spot. Don't be late. ⭐ 🤓 🌈 #constellationlife

El and Marcel each send me a thumbs-up and my heart slows.

I head back to Nana Billie and convince her to run into the cold water for a swim. Out in the swells, I spread my arms and legs and neck out as far and wide as I can until I am a floating star.

"THIS IS MY NATURAL HABITAT!" I sing into the never-ending blue. *"I BELONG HERE! I LIKE GIRLS!"*

"ME TOO!" Nana Billie's voice echoes, and then we laugh and flip around in the waves together. When we finally swim our way back to shore, our Black bodies glimmer like pearls in the sinking light.

Guess What's Coming to Dinner

BY MARK OSHIRO

EVERYTHING HAD TO be perfect.

Sofia knew that Mami would be home just as Papi finished making dinner, and she'd already taken care of *that*. "You have to make her favorite tonight," she told him when she plopped down at the table. She set her backpack on the floor. "Trust me. It's important."

Papi sat down opposite her. "Important, eh?" He smiled. "Do you have something planned?"

Sofia smiled right back. "Nope."

They both knew it was a lie, but one of the fun ones. The kind that her father let slide. So Papi rummaged about in the freezer to make Mami's favorite meal, and Sofia set out to make sure *nothing* was astray.

After all, it *had* to be perfect if this plan of hers was to work.

Sofia took her backpack to her room and placed it delicately at the foot of her bed, then dashed back downstairs. She sprayed and wiped the dining table, since she knew cleanliness was important. She laid out a setting for herself, Mami, and Papi, making sure the silverware was on the correct sides, and stepped back to examine it.

Nope. Her papi's place setting was crooked.

A moment later, she was satisfied. *There,* she thought. *Just as it needs to be.*

"Are you sure you're not planning anything?" Papi asked. Then he winked at her.

"Never," Sofia said, dancing away from one of his kisses. "Whatever makes you think I have something planned?"

"I know you, Sofia. I've seen you get this worked up before."

"I'm not worked up!"

Sofia's eyes went wide.

"Oh, I should go put on a nicer dress," she said, more to herself than to her papi.

"See?" he said. "You're worked up."

She stuck her tongue out.

It wasn't as though he was wrong.

IN HER BEDROOM, SOFIA SLIPPED ON HER
plum-colored dress, the one her mami said looked so good
with her brown, shadowed skin and her pale eyes. *Everything will be fine*, Sofia told herself, smoothing the fabric
against her legs. *You've thought of everything. You've done
your research. When you ask the question, they'll be in the
best possible mood, and it'll all work out.*

Sofia smiled at herself in the mirror on the back of her
door. She thought she looked pretty splendid, and she
twirled, the hem of her dress floating as she did so.

Yes, this was . . .

Perfect.

Mami was home not that much later, and Sofia was
there to greet her at the door and take her coat and her
cane. Her mother always took the fancy one to work and
used an old wooden one around the house. "Good evening, mija," Mami said, bending down to kiss Sofia's
forehead. "How was school?"

Sofia's heart fluttered. *You got this,* she told herself,
then took a deep breath.

"Fue bien, Mami," she said, and bowed dramatically.
"Your throne awaits, reina."

"A queen?" Mami laughed. "Today I am a *queen*?"

"You are *every* day," said Sofia as she took her mother's
hand and pulled her toward the kitchen. *Was that a little
too obvious?* she wondered.

"What's with all the ceremony?" Mami kissed Papi in the kitchen—Sofia allowed the brief detour—then sat at the head of the table. "Renato, did you make—"

"She insisted upon it," Papi said.

"Well," said Mami, "you've gone all out today, mija. What's the occasion?"

Sofia just smiled, hoping it covered up her nerves. She worried that if she spoke, it would ruin everything.

Papi served the food, and Sofia waited as her parents caught each other up on their days.

She waited.

And waited.

And then the lull came, and she knew this was it.

The perfect moment.

"Do you think I could invite a friend from school over for dinner this week?"

It was an innocent enough question, she thought. People did it all the time, right? Okay, maybe *they* weren't "people," so they hadn't done it, but . . . why not *now*? She'd started the sixth grade at a new school this year, and everyone—including Sofia—was worried that she wouldn't make friends. But she *had*. Angie's face popped into her head, and a warmth spread in her chest.

Papi's fork was halfway to his mouth when he froze. "What?" he said.

Mami closed her eyes for a moment. "Did I hear you correctly?"

"I think so," said Sofia. "Can I invite a friend and her family over for dinner this week? I was thinking . . . Friday?"

"Friday," Papi repeated. "As in . . . four days."

Mami raised a hand. "Cariño," she said to him, "I think there's a more pressing issue to address."

Sofia sat up a bit straighter. "I have been doing my research, Mami. Hours and hours of it. I've thought of *everything*."

"Everything?" Mami said. She shook her head. "Mija, that's a very big thing you are asking us."

"Well, I looked up meals," Sofia continued, holding out a finger for each thing she named. "And I know the perfect thing we can make. And I also read up about dinner customs and—"

"Sofia, that's lovely, but—" Papi began.

"—there's also this really nice postre we can serve at the end that her family would love and—"

Mami raised a hand. "Sofia, please," she said. "I'm so glad you did research, but we have to discuss more than just the details."

And then.

The words formed on her tongue.

Spilled from her mouth.

"I like her," Sofia blurted out.

Oh *no*.

This had not been part of her carefully calculated plan.

Why did you say that? She gripped the seat of her chair hard enough that one of her knuckles popped.

Mami and Papi exchanged a look.

"She likes her," Papi said.

"I heard," said Mami.

"Who is 'her,' mija?" asked Papi.

"Angie," said Sofia, hoping she could steer the conversation back to where she wanted it. She did not like losing control. "She's my best friend. From school."

"From the *new* school, right?" Papi asked. He nodded at Mami. "She actually made a friend, Claribel."

"Nuestra hija," Mami said back. "Out there making friends with—"

"I can *hear* you, you know," said Sofia, and sighed. "Angie is really important to me."

"That's wonderful!" said Mami.

"And we're both happy you've made a friend," added Papi. "But it's a big question to ask us. There are a lot of factors to consider. You know, ever since we moved into the neighborhood, we haven't had anyone like them over."

Sofia was prepared for that, too. "Well," she began, smiling ear to ear, "Angie asked her parents if it was possible, and they said yes, so that's already one step in the right direction."

"In the right direction?" Papi repeated. He smirked at Mami. "Did you hear that?"

"I did."

"What do you think?"

"It's a bold question," said Mami.

"Very."

"Do you think she's ready?"

"She's eleven," said Papi.

"Almost twelve!" exclaimed Sofia. Then, much quieter: "In seven months."

"Did you hear *that*?" Papi said, and Sofia wondered if they were making fun of her with the way they were talking.

"Almost *twelve*," said Mami. She crossed her arms over her chest. "Almost old enough to pay bills."

"And taxes."

"And vote."

"Practically *old* at this point."

"Maybe as old as us?"

The two of them giggled.

"You know I'm still sitting right here, right?" said Sofia.

"Shush, baby," said Papi, his light eyes playful. "The adults are talking."

"I think she's ready," said Mami.

"You do?"

"I do."

"But are *we* ready?" said Papi.

A hush fell over the table, and Sofia looked from one parent to the other. Again. And again. Neither of them were talking. Had she messed this up? Did they think she wasn't ready? Hadn't this all been *perfect*?

"We should talk as a family," said Mami. "We're very proud of how brave you're being. It's very admirable, mija. But there's more to it than that. We have to think about the right kind of food to serve—"

"Already on it, remember?" said Sofia, and she took out her phone. After a few moments of tapping on the screen, she passed it over to Mami. "I have multiple recipes we can practice the next couple of nights."

"We?" said Mami. "You're helping?"

"Isn't that fair?" Sofia scrunched up her face. "Since I'm the one asking for this?"

Mami's face softened. "Ay, mija, you really want this to happen, don't you?"

Sofia nodded.

Mami smiled. "Well, let me talk to your papi tonight.

Me and him. Then we can talk to you about it in the morning. Is that fair?"

Sofia beamed at her parents. "Of course! And I pulled up more stuff about customs, and there's this whole bit about the Accord we should probably read and—"

Papi put up a hand. "Later," he said. "Let's just enjoy dinner now, okay?"

Sofia was pleased with herself. It went better than she could have hoped. She kept stealing glances at her parents, and from the way they looked at one another, it seemed like they were having an entire conversation in their minds. Which wasn't even *possible*. They weren't like that.

"A girl," Papi finally said.

"I know," Mami said back.

The conversation moved on to other things, but deep inside, Sofia held on to the warm, fuzzy feeling that was slowly growing:

Hope.

SOFIA WAS READY TO GO TO SCHOOL A full forty-five minutes before she needed to be.

Today had to be perfect, too.

She wore her favorite overalls on top of a pink T-shirt,

then applied her daily makeup. It wasn't strictly necessary, and Mami had told her to be proud of her skin. "You should wear makeup only when you want to," she had explained. "We will support you either way."

So Sofia wore makeup most days, and that was because she had so much fun blending and contouring, matching shades with her outfits, experimenting with color as a means of expressing herself.

When she came downstairs, Papi was making breakfast—it smelled especially good this morning. She kissed him on the cheek when he leaned down for it, and then she started setting the table.

"Mija, es el desayuno," he said. "No need to set the table."

But she did anyway.

When Mami sat down, she seemed a little tired, and anxiety coursed through Sofia. Was this the wrong time? Were they not going to let Angie come over?

But after Papi served breakfast and Mami had some of her cafecito, Sofia's father reached over the table and took her hand. "You really wanted to impress us last night, didn't you?"

"Was I that obvious?" Sofia answered.

Mami yawned. "Only a little bit," she said. "But it helped. We know you're taking this seriously."

"I have the perfect meal to cook," Sofia said. "And we'll all be fine, I promise. Angie is so sweet, and her parents are, too. They are *very* progressive."

Mami took a deep breath. "This is really happening, isn't it?"

"I think so," said Papi.

"Does that mean . . . yes?" Sofia asked.

Her parents traded one last look.

"Yes, mija," said Mami, but before Sofia could move, Mami raised a hand. "We need to talk to Angie's parents *tonight*. No later. And if we don't feel like it's a good conversation or we don't feel safe with it just yet, we'll have to try another day."

"Oh, of course," Sofia said. "So you really mean it?"

"Yes," said Papi. He reached out and grabbed Mami's hand now. "We really do."

Sofia leapt up from the table and gave Mami and Papi each a hug. "Oh, gracias, gracias, gracias!" she exclaimed. "I promise you won't regret it!"

"I'm sure we won't," said Papi.

"Right," said Mami.

They were both quieter than usual the rest of breakfast, but Sofia didn't make much of it.

"THEY ACTUALLY SAID YES?" ANGIE'S MOUTH
fell open. "Really?"

"They *did*," said Sofia, and she couldn't help it. They grabbed hands and began to jump up and down, screaming the whole time. Sofia didn't even care that there were other kids staring at them, at least not at first. One of them, Brian Winco, stared a little too long, brushed his blond hair out of his face, and then howled at them before running off.

"Ignore him," said Angie. "He's always weird like that."

Sofia laughed. "You'd think there was a full moon or something."

Angie guided Sofia over to one of the benches near the basketball court, and they both sat down. "Okay," she said. "I have to tell my parents as soon as I get home so that they can call your parents." She paused. "Oh, wow. I'll get to come over in *three days*."

Three days. It didn't seem real! This was the first time that *anyone* who wasn't family had come over since Sofia's family had moved after the Accord, so . . . was that enough time? Three days to prepare?

"My parents will probably be all annoying and whatever on the phone," Sofia warned, suddenly nervous. "But I think they're fine. They're just . . . a little nervous, I guess."

Angie raised an eyebrow. "Is it . . . is it because of *us*?"

Sofia let go of Angie's hand. "I don't know. I think it's all so new to them that they don't know what to do."

"But . . . they said yes, right?"

When Angie smiled, it lit up her whole face, and right then, it was like she was the sun itself. Sofia needed that. It was a reminder of why she was taking this risk.

"You're right," said Sofia. "It's going to be just fine!"

No.

Sofia was going to make sure it was *perfect*.

AFTER SOFIA FINISHED HER HOMEWORK ON Wednesday afternoon, she spent hours looking up recipes. This was a special occasion. This was *important*. But what if the food wasn't good? Or Angie's family didn't like it?

She asked her mami about it over dinner that night, but her mother was dismissive. "I know you're probably nervous, but it'll be fine," Mami said. "It hasn't been *that* long since I last cooked a meal like this. I think between me and your father, we'll be fine."

"But what if she *hates* it?"

"Hates the meal?" Papi tilted his head. "Sofia, I don't think—"

"It's possible," she said. "And then Angie will run away screaming and tell all her friends that we're freaks and—"

Mami put her fork down so hard that it clanged against the plate. "Mija, no," she said, practically spitting out the last word. "We don't refer to ourselves that way, okay?"

"I know," Sofia said. "But what if *others* do?"

Papi sighed. "Your friend Angie," he said, "her parents called not too long ago. We had a long talk with them."

"Really?" Sofia put her own fork down. "Was it okay?"

He smiled. "Your friend really likes you, doesn't she?"

Sofia tried to hide her bashfulness, but her mami laughed. "I'm guessing that's a yes," said Mami. "And you like her."

"Something like that," Sofia said quietly, trying to avoid *both* her parents staring at her.

"They *want* to come here, mija," said Papi, caressing the back of her hand. "If they thought that about you or us, they wouldn't bother showing up."

"So the call was . . . fine?"

A grin spread across Papi's face. "You could say that."

"Papiiii," Sofia whined. "You're not helping."

Mami laughed. "Angie's parents were very kind," she said. "I think they were concerned about us as much as we were about them."

"Because this is so *new*," Papi said quickly. "Not because of who you are. They know Angie really likes you. Apparently, she talks about you all the time, too."

Sofia's cheeks went hot. The idea of that felt . . . well, it felt really good.

"They're very excited to be here on Friday," Mami continued. "And they trust us to cook as well! It's going to be fine, mija."

"You think so?" said Sofia.

"Absolutely," said Mami. "I think it will be a very special gathering for all of us. Your father and I will both cook the best meal possible, and everything will be just fine."

Sofia hoped so.

BY THE TIME FRIDAY ARRIVED, SOFIA HAD never felt so nervous in her entire life.

Yet Angie seemed . . . exactly the same. They greeted one another with a hug at the start of the day, and Angie walked Sofia to her first class. "I'm so excited for tonight!" she said before leaving Sofia and running off to make it to her class on time.

Okay, thought Sofia. *She seems happy.*

At lunch, their routine didn't change either. They met

up at the doors to the cafeteria, and Angie's fingers found Sofia's hand and held it. She kept it that way all through the line, chatting away about her day. They passed the table full of most of the football team, and Brian woofed and howled at the two of them.

"He's such a doofus," said Angie.

And then she squeezed Sofia's hand tighter.

Like it was a promise.

Maybe Sofia was overthinking this. She got worked up when things weren't the way she wanted them to be. But Angie wasn't acting weird around her. It was like any other day!

Still.

Everything *had* to be perfect that night.

Because what if it wasn't?

This whole situation was new, and it was strange. It was weird enough feeling like she did about Angie, but what if the dinner went horribly? What if Angie's family came over and they *hated* the food? What if all the preparation didn't matter once these people were in their home and saw what kind of family they were? What if they never wanted their daughter to see Sofia again?

It was all a big unknown. And it scared Sofia. She just wanted to know: Was this going to be a disaster?

Sofia rushed home after school and greeted her papi, who was working at the kitchen table. He tried to ask her about her day, but she held up a hand. "Later," she said. "I have to get ready." She couldn't predict the future, but there were some things she *could* control. This was one of them.

He looked at the clock on the stove. "Mija, it's like . . . three-thirty. No one will be here until seven."

She put her hands on her hips and shook her head. "True art takes time."

"Okay, okay," he said, returning to the papers spread out on the table. "Got the message."

He looked up.

Winked at her.

"Go get 'em," he said. "Make me proud."

And then she was off! She ran to her room and closed the door, then pulled *everything* out of her closet: every dress, every skirt, every blouse. The dress pants that Mami got her after that big government ceremony for the Accord. The distressed jeans she had found at a thrift store and been meaning to use in an outfit. Not tonight, though. No, it would have to be *truly* special for tonight.

Sofia set aside a skirt she loved more than anything: black with tiny yellow stars all over it. Once she laid it out on the bed, she knew what would go with it: a long-sleeve black top. And her moon necklace! Yes, this was perfect.

Perfect.

Sofia showered, taking time to relax under the hot water.

And then she had to make her decision.

After her shower, Sofia dressed. Her outfit looked spectacular, and she was so happy she had chosen that skirt and top. But . . . should she wear makeup?

She wore it to school every day, but that was different. Lots of people did. Here at home, though, she almost *never* did. Why would she? She had no one to impress.

She still loved the feeling of wearing makeup, and that was one reason to wear it tonight. But what was the right decision? What was . . . *perfect?*

She wandered downstairs, where Papi and Mami were busy in the kitchen. Papi stirred something on the stove while Mami chopped up vegetables.

Mami was the first to realize that Sofia was standing at a distance. She turned. "¿Estás bien, mija?" she asked. "What is it?" She looked down at Sofia's hands, which held a bottle of foundation. "Do you need help?"

Sofia laughed. "No, Mami," she said. "I know how to do it. I just wondered . . . *should* I do it?"

Papi stopped stirring. "Do you *want* to?"

"I don't know," she said. "I don't normally wear it at home."

"Then do what you feel is right," said Mami. "I wasn't going to wear any. Neither was your papi. Now we can do it together."

That was *exactly* what Sofia needed. No makeup, then. If her mami could do it, so could she.

THE DOORBELL RANG AT 6:55 P.M.

Sofia felt a rush through her body, like her emotions were racing one another to be the first thing she felt in her heart. Fear. Joy. Terror. Happiness. Instead, she experienced it all: it was a storm in her chest.

It was finally happening.

Would she survive the night?

Angie stepped in first. She'd pulled her hair tight into two long braids that hung down her back. She was wearing yellow, and it popped against her dark brown skin. *Wow,* thought Sofia. *I've never seen her like this.*

"Sofia!" Angie exclaimed, and then she sprang forward and held her in a hug.

She stopped.

Stepped back.

"Wow, you look *ah-mazing*!" Angie said. "Look at that skirt! And your hair! And we technically are matching with yellow!"

Then Angie looked into her eyes.

Into a face *without* makeup.

And said:

"You're really pretty, Sofia."

She raised her hand and ran a thumb over Sofia's cheek, and her smile was so warm, so perfect.

And just like that . . . it washed over Sofia.

Relief.

"Thank you," she said, and then she looked Angie up and down. "And look who's talking!"

Angie played up the drama and acted bashful. "Oh, *stop*."

She stepped aside, and her fathers—Craig and Damone—came inside holding hands. The adults greeted one another, and Sofia guided Angie to the dining room. "You're gonna sit here," she said, pointing to one of the six empty chairs.

"Why there?" Angie asked.

"So that I can sit next to you," Sofia answered.

Angie's face lit up with a smile. "Oh. *Duh*. Of course!"

"You girls just gonna run off and not introduce yourselves?" Papi said, coming into the room and acting scandalized. "Sofia, where *are* your manners?"

"Sorry!" she said. "I just got excited."

"No worries," said Damone. He sniffed. "Yo, what smells so *good* in here?"

It was Mami's turn to smile. "We teamed up for this meal," she said, grabbing Papi's hand. "We actually haven't cooked food like this in a couple of years, you know?"

"Turns out she remembers how to make pozole from memory," Papi added. "And I made some fresh tortillas, too. Abuela's recipe."

Angie took her seat. "But . . . what are *you* going to eat?" she asked.

"Mami made two pots of pozole," Sofia said. "As long as ours has brains in it, we can eat pretty much everything else."

"Ohhh," Angie said. "That makes sense!"

"I still can't believe what the school gets away with serving every day," said Papi. "It's all so *bland.*"

"So you do your shopping at the Wegmans over on Atlantic, right?" Damone asked. "I hear their selection of brains is a lot more diverse. Different species and whatnot."

Mami smiled. "We *do*! There's a corner market down the street if we need a quick fix, but we prefer the fresher stuff."

"Oh, well, y'all got to come over to our place next

time," said Craig, sitting across from Sofia and next to his husband. "My family is from Mississippi; Damone's is from Alabama. And he can mix up a mean pot of greens using brains instead of ham hocks."

Mami and Papi brought the pot of pozole and the fixings to the table, and then . . . silence. Sofia swallowed loudly and looked around the table.

Wow, she thought. *This is really happening.*

Mami served bowls of the steaming soup, and aside from quiet thanks and small talk, no one really said anything. Sofia took her own bowl and began to blow on it, hoping it would cool down soon. She was *hungry,* and that itch in the back of her mind was starting to come forth.

"So . . . this is new for us," said Damone. "I know we talked about it on the phone."

"Us too," said Papi. "You're the first to visit us."

"Like . . . *ever?*" said Craig. He tried a bit of the burning hot pozole and immediately appeared to regret it.

"Careful, Daddy!" said Angie. "Can't you see it's steaming?"

"He's always been the impatient type," said Damone.

"Sounds like Claribel," said Papi, and then he winked at Sofia.

"An-y-way," said Craig, dragging the word out. "We're glad our daughter has found a friend in Sofia."

"We feel the same way," said Mami. "I'm glad for the Species Accord, but it hasn't made humans that eager to hang out with us. There are still people who think all zombies do is eat other humans."

"Well, *we* don't think that," said Angie. "It never happened before anyway. People just think all the stories are true and *I* know they're not."

Damone smiled. "I mean, we've all heard stories growing up, but like we said on the phone . . . people used to tell stories about two men marrying one another all the time. So we kinda get it."

"And if it wasn't for the Accord, Sofia woulda never come here," said Angie. "So . . . that's good." And she smiled at Sofia, her face lighting up.

Sofia turned from Angie for a moment as the others continued talking, and she caught her papi staring at her, a funny look on his face, his chin resting in his palm. She wanted to ask him about it, but he reached out and rubbed her arm. "Te amo, mija," he said, his voice soft, floating just under the conversation.

Everything felt right.

She turned back toward Angie, but it was her mami who caught her attention this time. Her mouth was open wide. "You never mentioned that on the phone!"

"Mentioned what?" Sofia asked.

"One of my aunts was turned years ago," said Da-mone. "And Auntie Myra is one of Angie's favorite peo-ple in the world."

"*Turned?*" said Sofia. "You never told me there was a zombie in your family!"

"She just . . . never came up," said Angie. "There are a couple of werewolves and vampires, too!"

"Wow, this is *really* good," said Craig, and Sofia turned to see him shoveling spoonfuls of pozole—all clearly too hot—into his mouth. "What is it called again?"

As the grown-ups veered into another conversation, Sofia felt something under the table.

Angie's hand.

"Thank you for inviting me," said Angie. "Every-thing feels so . . . so *perfect.*"

Sofia melted. "I'm glad you're here," she said.

"Me too."

Sofia squeezed her hand back.

A promise.

And right then, Sofia did not feel like one of the undead.

No, she felt *very* much alive.

the GOLEM and the MAPMAKER
by MOLLY KNOX OSTERTAG
If I lose the Princess, I will have failed.
I cannot let that happen.

Huf Huf

I'm not supposed to let my runes get wet. Please don't do that again.

And don't try to run, either.

What would you do?

Hurt me?

What?! No. I couldn't.

Aren't you some kind of magic soldier?

Hurting people is your job.

I am a *golem*. Made of clay and arcana, bound to the will of the Emperor. I fight if he commands me to. But my current command is to escort you to his palace for your wedding. —

Safely.

Why do you keep running away from me?

I'm eighteen, I don't need an annoying babysitter!

But as we travel,
I try my best to care
for the Princess.

So she will not
find me "annoying."

It's almost night!

I'm too tired.

We can wait 'til tomorrow.

As you say, my lady.

CLINK

What are you—

I never wanted anything else.

But now —

Princess! Are you ready? The ceremony is beginning!

Coming!

The Wish &
the Wind Dragon

BY KATHERINE LOCKE

WHEN JUPITER REACHED the crow's nest, they flopped against the side, catching their breath. Sweat slicked their forehead, and they wiped their reddish-brown bangs away from their face and out of their eyes. They needed a haircut. Badly. They liked to keep it long on one side and short on the other, but after months at sea, it had grown out, choppy and uneven. They hated it. Maybe Luna would cut their hair for the holiday. If they ever made it home for the holiday.

Jupiter's family's ship, the *Lovely Belle,* was miles and miles and *miles* from their family's secret cove in the Pearl Islands, where their ships came together once a year to celebrate the summer solstice. Ever since Jupiter's sister, Luna, and her wife, Azura, got their own ship last year, Jupiter hadn't seen them *once,* and now, without any wind, they might miss the summer solstice gathering. They might not see them until next year.

And anything could happen in a year.

It wasn't like being a family of pirates was a risk-free occupation.

Jupiter knew exactly what Luna would say if Luna were here in this crow's nest with them. Luna would say, *Stop worrying! Pirates don't worry so much!* But worrying was what Jupiter did. Jupiter was a very good worrier. They were almost as good a worrier as they were a pirate.

And sometimes worrying was helpful. Jupiter's worrying made them check all the supplies before they left their last port and that's the only way anyone would have found out that all their rice had bugs in it. They would've starved on the seas without it, but because of Jupiter's worrying and checking, their parents were able to buy more rice before they left.

But right now, worrying felt heavy. It felt like it could pull Jupiter right through the floor of this crow's nest. It was a cannonball in their chest.

When this happened, Luna always told them to touch something, and smell something, and look at something, and listen for something. So that's what Jupiter did.

Jupiter touched the rough wood of the crow's nest.

Sometimes people got splinters up here, if they weren't very careful.

Jupiter smelled the scent of the sea. When it was quiet like this, it wasn't quite as salty as when it was windy. It was briny, like salt and fish had sat in a tub of water out in the heat.

Jupiter peered over the edge of the crow's nest at the wide, glittering sea. There weren't any waves, and there weren't any birds. The sea stretched in every direction as far as they could see, alternating dark and light where the sunlight hit it, until it turned as white as a diamond at the horizon from all the sunlight. It was midsummer after all.

And Jupiter listened. The sails were down because there was no point in having sails up without wind. So all they could hear was the sound of people below, scrubbing the decks and cleaning the cannons, all the tasks of a bored crew that Jupiter's mother, the matriarch of the ship, desperately wanted to keep busy.

They needed wind.

They needed wind because a bored crew started fights and argued with each other. The heat made everyone testy, but the heat and nothing to do made them riotous.

They needed wind because pirates—or anyone who sailed ships—couldn't do their work without it.

They needed wind because Jupiter wanted to get home to the solstice celebration and to their sister.

Jupiter's eyes searched the sky, but there were no clouds, and no shadows high above. No birds, and no wind dragons. Wind dragons were rare beings, dragons who blew air instead of flame and lived along coastlines. When they fought, there were storms. When the wind dragon clans warred, there were hurricanes. But when a wind dragon was near, sailors who flew under all flags could ask the wind dragon to blow in their favor.

When the wind had first died down, Jupiter's mother sent one of her sailors to the crow's nest to scour the skies for wind dragons, and that night, in their cabin, Jupiter watched her make a wish.

But no wind dragon arrived.

That had been a few nights ago. Perhaps a wind dragon hadn't been nearby to hear the wish. Wishes could only travel so far, and not every wish was granted. Especially by dragons.

Jupiter's hands searched their pants pockets and pulled out a small candle and flint. Fire was dangerous on a ship, but they only needed a little bit of smoke to make this wish.

They gripped the candle. Maybe there was a dragon nearby this time. There was no harm in wasting a wish, of course, but there was always a risk that another kind of dragon could hear it. The kind of dragon who might want to eat them and burn their sails instead of blowing them toward the islands.

Jupiter could worry all day about this. But they remembered what their mother always said: *A wish is always worth making, like a risk is always worth taking.*

They struck the fire starter, and the wick of the candle caught. They blew it out immediately, catching the smoke in their hand.

When they released it, they whispered, "I wish for a wind dragon."

The smoke curled into the air, gray and twisting, like a dragon coming out of the sea, until it disappeared against the blue sky.

The candle wax dripped onto Jupiter's hand.

They waited.

IT WAS HIGH NOON OF THE FOLLOWING

day, and Jupiter's mother had set them to work repairing sails. When it was windy, or they had sailed through a storm, the force of the air could rend small tears in the sails. Today, Jupiter was mending the spritsail, the square sail that sat off the bow of the ship. It'd been torn a few weeks ago when they'd sailed through a bad storm off the coast of Aega.

Jupiter thought about sitting on the deck to do the work, but their mother thought they'd be in the way, so had sent them belowdecks. They sat in her office beneath the quarterdeck, surrounded by her telescopes and her maps and her measuring tools, and they secretly didn't mind. It was a little cooler down here than it was up in the full sun. One of the *Lovely Belle*'s two cats, Miri, slept on the chair next to them, her paws twitching in a dream.

Jupiter hummed a soft sea shanty to themself as they worked, the thick needle going in and out of the heavy cotton weave, and they were so engrossed that they almost missed the shout from above.

They paused, their needle halfway through the sail, and listened.

There was another indistinct shout, and then footsteps pounding above Jupiter's head. Jupiter couldn't make out the words but wanted to know what was going on. They didn't hear any gunfire, but it could be another ship overtaking them. They took a deep breath and practiced dismissing the thought. If they were caught in a windless stretch of time, so was everyone else who might have reason to capture the *Lovely Belle*. Jupiter knew their mother would want them to stay belowdecks, but curiosity, and the desperate need to know it *wasn't* another ship, got the best of them.

They put down the sail, the needle and the thread,

and sneaked by the still-sleeping cat. In the hallway, Jupiter was nearly bowled over by Amra, one of the young crew members who was Jupiter's friend. She was taller than Jupiter by a lot, even though she was only two years older than them, and one of the best sailors Jupiter had ever seen. She was stronger than she looked and Jupiter had once seen her catch a loose cannon and roll it back into position, lashing it down to the deck, all on her own during a gun battle.

"What is it?" Jupiter called.

"Someone's seen a dragon!" Amra called over her shoulder. She cocked them a lazy grin.

The last time Jupiter had seen a dragon was six months ago, just after the New Year. A shadow had crossed the full moon on a very cold winter night on one of the northern seas. Their mother had let them watch the dragon through one of her telescopes, and Jupiter could see the way the moonlight glinted off the dragon's scales.

But that had been a mountain dragon, migrating as they often did from snow-covered mountain range to snow-covered mountain range.

What if this one was a fire dragon, come to eat them?

Jupiter bit their lip.

It could be a fire dragon. But what if it was a wind dragon, like they'd wished for?

Jupiter had never seen a wind dragon.

And, more importantly, Jupiter had never had a wish come true when they needed it the most. Silly wishes, little wishes, yes, but never big ones, and never ones granted by a dragon. Wish magic was a precarious magic—and wishes didn't always come true, for reasons the wisher would never know.

They raced after Amra and climbed the ladder behind her, their hands and feet moving so fast they were sure they'd slip and fall, embarrassing themself as a child who'd grown up on the ships, but then Amra was pulling them up onto the deck, her hand warm and tight around their own. They joined the growing crew standing in the hot summer sun, looking up at the dragon circling high overhead.

In the middle of the deck stood Jupiter's mother and father. Their mother stood with her captain's cloak on, a rich navy blue like a night sky and scattered with stars for all of the ships they held in their clan, one of her smaller telescopes to her eye. Jupiter's father, the ship's navigator, stood to her side without his family cloak on. He scratched at his beard, glancing between the dragon and the telescope. He caught Jupiter's eye and gave them a reassuring wink.

"It's a wind dragon," announced the captain, relief in her voice.

A few members of the crew cheered, but the rest

watched the dragon in silence with upturned, hopeful faces. It hadn't dropped low enough to give them a gift of wind.

Jupiter's mother looked around. "We're a long way from shore." That was where wind dragons usually lived, in the rocky cliffs off the coasts. "Did anyone call a wind dragon?"

Jupiter sucked in a breath. Next to them, Amra's head jerked at the sound and she elbowed them. "Was it you? Speak up!"

Would Jupiter get in trouble? Calling on a dragon for something like this? Sailing was about patience, and calling on a dragon was the absolute opposite of patience. Plus, perhaps their mother would consider it a wasted wish, a frivolous wish. Perhaps no one else was worried about getting home in time.

"Jupiter!" hissed Amra. She was looking at them, wide-eyed, like she knew. Maybe it was written all over their face. Maybe she'd seen the smoke from their candle up there in the crow's nest.

Jupiter swallowed hard. They had to say *something* or Amra would. "I wished for the wind dragon."

It felt like the entire crew, all fifty eyes, turned toward them. It made Jupiter's knees shake to have that many people looking at them. But they lifted their chin and said it louder. "I was the one who wished for the wind dragon, Captain."

Their mother's mouth quirked at the corner. She studied them for a long beat, then said, "So you were. A wished-for dragon only responds to the wisher, Jupiter. You'll have to climb up there and call to it."

Jupiter swallowed. They didn't want to be that close to a wind dragon. "It won't just know what I want?"

The captain softened, transforming from the captain to their mother in a blink. She stepped toward them and ran a light hand over their head, ruffling their hair. "No, you'll have to ask. You can do it, my love."

Jupiter wanted to lean into her touch and ask her if she'd climb up there with them. They didn't want to have to speak to a dragon face to face all by themself. But they would, if they had to.

They looked at the faces of the hopeful crew. They wiped their sweaty hands on their rough trousers. They listened to the stillness of the sea and the ship. They breathed in the briny air.

They'd wished for the dragon. They could do this.

Above them, a sky-blue wind dragon circled almost lazily in the air. Jupiter grabbed the rungs of the mast ladder and began to climb. Halfway up, their arms burned and their legs burned, and they kept having to stop to carefully wipe one hand at a time against their shirt.

But when they reached the crow's nest, they felt . . . exhilaration. That was the word for the crackling like a firecracker inside their chest. The sheer excitement and anxiety and joy of doing something they hadn't done before. Wishing for a wind dragon. They'd wished on many things before, but they'd been silly and small things—more gifts at solstice, or for their mother to let them play instead of working. This had been the first time they'd wished for something big, and important, and it had come true.

They lay on their back for a second, just to catch their breath and summon the courage they needed to face the wind dragon. And in that second, they heard the sound of boots on the ladder. They rolled over, sticking their face through the hole in the bottom of the crow's nest. Amra was climbing up, her skirts swishing side to side with every determined step, exposing the trousers she wore beneath them.

"Hey," she whispered, a little out of breath. "You're in my way."

Jupiter scrambled away from the hole so Amra could make her way into the crow's nest. She sat against the side, stretching her legs out. Her chest rose and fell again and again as she caught her breath.

"Been *ages* since I came up here," she said, her eyes closed. "I forgot how *high* it was."

"It's very high" was the only thing Jupiter could manage to say.

Amra cracked open one eye and grinned at them. "Thought you'd want company when you spoke to the dragon."

Now that they were up there, Jupiter did not want company. Jupiter wanted the option of embarrassing themself without an audience. But Jupiter also liked the idea of Amra seeing them do something bold and brave, something that Amra herself had never done before.

They swallowed and climbed to their feet, gripping the side of the crow's nest. How did one even call to a dragon? They thought about it for a minute and thought about how someone in a story might call to a dragon. Below-decks at night, when the crew traded stories and built off them, a tradition amongst seafolk, they had heard stories of people who spoke to, and even rode, dragons.

They cleared their throat and then called into the sky, "I am the wisher."

The sun crawled across the sky, like a cat stretching to wake up from a nap. Slowly, without a rush, all length and shadows.

On the deck, the crew watched.

Beside Jupiter, Amra held her breath.

And in the sky, the dragon circled.

Jupiter waited.

Abruptly, the dragon's wings pinned to its sides and it dove down, toward the ship. On the deck, the crew yelled, and Jupiter heard their mother call loudly, "No weapons! Trust!"

Jupiter gripped the edge of the crow's nest, holding on and trying to do just that: trust. Trust that their mother was right and the dragon wouldn't attack them. Trust that the dragon was simply getting closer. Trust that this dragon would grant them the wish.

At the last moment, the dragon beat its enormous wings forward in a powerful, sweeping motion, breaking its dive. The gust of wind knocked Jupiter backward, nearly into the hole in the floor of the crow's nest, but Amra caught them and helped them back up. The ship rocked back and forth.

Jupiter exhaled as they faced the dragon.

The dragon was pale blue, the color of most wind dragons they'd seen in books, with shimmery scales that caught the light and reflected it. Their wings looked leathery and wrinkly, like Jupiter's grandmother's hands, and they beat up and down like a heartbeat, keeping the dragon hovering close to the crow's nest. The dragon was not enormous, perhaps about half the size of the *Lovely Belle*, but they seemed bigger up here, facing Jupiter.

Their eye was catlike, amber, and enormous, and all too knowing.

You are the wisher?

Jupiter felt the question in their chest more than heard it with their ears.

They swallowed. "I am the wisher."

The dragon's lips pulled back. *You must learn how to wish better.*

Jupiter blinked at them. "What did I do wrong?"

The dragon made a noise close to a sigh. *You wished for me, not for the wind I make.*

Dread flooded Jupiter's stomach like a breach in the hull. "I—I didn't think of that."

The dragon blinked. *I know.*

"Would you," whispered Jupiter, "consider granting the wish I should have made?"

The dragon eyed them. *You could make a great many wishes. But this is the one you want.*

Jupiter nodded.

The dragon's wings rose and fell, lifting their body into the air, fighting against the gravity of the world, the way Jupiter fought against the worry and embarrassment weighing their body down.

If the dragon didn't grant them the wish, if the whole crew saw a wind dragon come and go without providing the wind, they'd know that Jupiter had messed up the wish. They'd know Jupiter had failed. And Jupiter would never reach Luna.

Jupiter swallowed back a lump in their throat.

Then the dragon spoke. *Very well. You'll want your sails up for this. I'll give you the wind you need. When you are ready, wave at me.*

And with a flick of their tail and a tilt of their wings, the dragon swooped down toward the sea before beating their wings and rising into the sky again.

Jupiter collapsed onto the floor of the crow's nest, pressing their hands to their sternum. Their heart pounded against their palms.

"Oh my sea gods," gasped Amra, scooting over. Her dark eyes were wide as barrels. "What happened?"

"You couldn't hear them?" Jupiter asked.

Amra shook her head. "Just what you were saying!"

"They're going to give us the wind," said Jupiter faintly, in disbelief. "We need to run up the sails."

Amra scrambled to her feet and leaned over the side of the crow's nest. "SAILS!"

And on the deck, the captain echoed her call. "Sails!"

There was a flurry of activity below the crow's nest, but Jupiter could only stay very, very still.

Amra crouched beside them. "Are you well? Did the dragon harm you?"

Jupiter shook their head, still trying to breathe. "Amra."

"What?" She looked worried.

"I talked to a *dragon*," they whispered.

Amra grinned. "Yes, you did. Come on. Let's go down. We don't want to be up here when the dragon starts blowing."

Amra went first down the ladder, with Jupiter following right after. Jupiter concentrated on the movement of their hands and their feet searching for the next rung. The rhythm soothed the shakiness in their muscles and the hurricane in their mind. A *dragon*. A real wind dragon heard their wishes and *came*! Jupiter had only heard stories of it happening. They'd never seen it with their own two eyes. They weren't sure if they knew anyone who had seen it with their own two eyes.

Did it *mean* anything? Jupiter wasn't sure whether they wanted to know.

When they hit the deck, the crew swarmed them.

"What did it sound like?"

"How did you talk to it?"

"How'd you do it?"

"Sure it's not going to attack us?"

"Why didn't you do this days ago?"

Then one voice rose above the fray. "Let them be! Get back to work!"

Jupiter's father reached through the crowd and settled a hand on their shoulder, shifting his body between them and the rest of the crew. He leaned down and whispered, "Go to the quarterdeck. Your mother wants you."

Jupiter's heart squeezed. Was their mother angry? She'd seemed proud, but perhaps something went wrong. Perhaps they'd asked for the wrong thing.

But then their father gave them a warm smile and a wink. "Well done, Jupiter. A wish—"

"—is always worth making, like a risk is always worth taking," Jupiter finished, grinning.

"Never forget that," said their father.

Jupiter straightened their shoulders and headed for the quarterdeck. That was where their parents were most of the days, when their mother wasn't walking and talking to the crew. Their father could always, always be found there, or in the cabins below, where he pored over maps the way some people pored over books. Jupiter didn't get to go up to the quarterdeck often, and every time they did, they felt important and special.

Right then, they felt the most important, and the most special, they ever had. But they were still shaking. As they walked up the steps, they glanced into the sky at the wind dragon, who was circling around toward them again. The sails were almost fully up, and their mother was watching the progress with her hands folded behind her back.

She glanced down at Jupiter, giving them her private little smile again. "Hello, wisher."

Jupiter flushed. "I'm sorry."

"Don't be," said their mother reassuringly. "I am proud of you, and glad that we have a wind dragon. What do we need to do?"

Jupiter wasn't used to that question from their mother. "When the sails are up, they asked me to wave at them."

Their mother nodded to the full white-and-tan sails. "They're up. Whenever you're ready."

Jupiter took a deep breath, went to the rail of the ship, and looked up at the dragon. It soared steadily, as if it could find wind in the air that the rest of them could not feel.

Jupiter lifted their arm, tentatively at first, and then vigorously, waving back and forth as if they were signaling for help. And in a way, they were. *If this doesn't work . . .*

The dragon's wings rose and fell, and the dragon's body tilted toward the *Lovely Belle.* They came closer, and closer, and still there was no wind. Jupiter's bottom lip trembled. Maybe wind dragons could run out of wind. They hadn't thought of that possibility. Maybe the wind dragon used so much wind coming across the sea that there was no more wind inside of them and—just then, the dragon opened their mouth.

Rows of glinting white teeth.

A long purplish-black tongue like Jupiter had once seen on a giraffe.

And then *WHOOSH!*

The wind hit the sails so hard the ship leapt forward, plunging toward the water. Everyone shouted as it rose back up, charging forward again. Jupiter's mother dove into action, shouting instructions for sails to be lowered and changed. Jupiter's father was down on the deck, his hands wrapped around a rope that he held taut for someone to tie off. Jupiter turned to the dragon, who was still blowing on them.

"Thank you!" they called.

The dragon didn't say anything, but Jupiter thought they could feel their response, warm and appreciative of the acknowledgment.

The wish wind steadied, and the ship steadied, and suddenly they were charging across the water, swift as they'd ever traveled on a clear day, toward the Pearl Islands, summer solstice, and Jupiter's sister and sister-in-law.

THEY SAILED ALL THROUGH THE DAY, WITH the shadow of the dragon covering half the ship and the sound of its wings nearly as loud as the sound of the wind against the taut sails. The dragon blew wind, and the *Lovely Belle* sailed until the wind died down, and then the dragon blew again. Over and over. They sailed through the short, nearly solstice night, and through the next day. And just around supper, one of the sailors on the foredeck called, "Land ahoy!"

A cheer went up from the crew. Jupiter and Amra were belowdecks, helping the cook with the dishes, when they heard the cry. Amra grabbed Jupiter's hand, dragging them up to the deck. Just on the edge of the sea, right where the sun turned bright red and bled into the water, Jupiter could make out the dark, rocky shore of the Pearl Islands, and to the north, at the cove, the white sails of ships.

Luna, thought Jupiter, giddy with excitement. They'd done it. They'd get to see their sister.

"The dragon!" exclaimed Amra.

Jupiter turned and saw that the dragon was pulling away from the ship. The dragon had looked tired this morning, when they were flying above the ship, and they had taken no breaks in providing the wind needed on the too-still sea. They'd gone above and beyond, in Jupiter's mind, in providing the wind they'd wished for.

Jupiter ran up the stairs to the quarterdeck and to the edge of the railing.

"Dragon!" they called.

The dragon turned their head toward Jupiter. *Yes, wisher?*

"Thank you," said Jupiter. "Thank you very, very much."

The dragon's joy rippled through Jupiter like warm, dappled sunlight. *You're welcome, wisher. I am glad I heard your wish.*

"Me too," Jupiter said, but the dragon was already gone, a dark speck in the sky glimmering in the sun.

BY THE TIME THEY ACTUALLY MADE IT INTO the cove, dropped anchor, and organized themselves to row to shore, it was hours later, and Jupiter was exhausted. Their *bones* felt tired inside their skin, like they were heavier with every minute.

"Stay awake," their mother said. "Luna's onshore and I bet she's excited to see you."

Jupiter was not going to fall asleep before they saw their sister. Not after all this. They scanned the shoreline, where the village was alight with burning torches and lanterns, colorful banners and garlands draped everywhere, and they could hear the distant sound of music—guitars, drums, bells. There were people on the beach, and people up into the village, and all the ships still had skeleton crews to guard them, so people waved as the crew from the *Lovely Belle* rowed past. Even the ships had rainbow garlands hanging from their railings and masts.

The rowboat bumped into the dock, and Amra scurried out to tie it up. She offered a hand to Jupiter, but Jupiter was already climbing onto the dock and scrambling to their feet.

A familiar woman was striding down the beach toward the docks. Her boots clicked on the rock path, and her long red hair was pulled back in a sensible braid. Behind her, another woman, shorter and with cropped hair, hurried to catch up.

"Luna!" called Jupiter.

"Jupiter!" called Luna back, joy bursting like fireworks through her voice.

She ran down the dock and Jupiter ran to her. Luna swept Jupiter up in a huge hug, spinning them around and setting them down on their feet.

"Look at you!" Luna said, gripping Jupiter's shoulders. "You're growing like a wave."

"They're going to catch up to you, Lune," teased Luna's wife, Azura, coming up and giving Jupiter a big hug too.

"Oh no, Jupiter," said Luna gravely. "If you do that, I'll have to throw you overboard."

Jupiter was not entirely sure if Luna was kidding, even when Luna and Azura started laughing.

"Jupiter," Amra said, appearing behind them, "did you tell them about the dragon?"

"What dragon?" Luna said. "What kind of dragon?"

"They wished, and a wind dragon came. Otherwise we never would have made it here," Amra said proudly.

Luna looked at Jupiter, eyebrows raised. "Oh, is that right? A wind dragon? Of course you did, Jupiter. Come on, you'll have to tell me about it. You know I've never seen one?"

She and Azura started to lead Jupiter away, but Jupiter stopped. "Amra should come too. She tells stories much better than I do."

Luna gave Jupiter another arched eyebrow and glanced at her wife. Azura smiled. "Of course. I know that feeling well. Come on, Amra. Help Jupiter tell us about their wish and the wind dragon."

And so, as they started to walk toward their clan's secret village, with its music and its food and its solid ground and Jupiter's family all around them, Jupiter began their story.

"I wanted to see you," they said simply. "And there was no wind."

Splinter & Ash

BY MARIEKE NIJKAMP

IN THE CITY of Haven, most people were who other people expected them to be.

And to most people, I was a whole lot of things. Du-Lac's unfortunate youngest who was wild at heart. And: destined for the Convent of the Fields. Oh, and don't forget: that wretched girl who punched the prince.

But the prince was a bully. And I was no girl. And maybe I was DuLac's unfortunate youngest and wild at heart, but I didn't plan to go to any convent. That plan was my uncle's, if I didn't show that I knew how to be a proper lady. Whatever *that* meant.

I wanted to be someone else. I dreamed of becoming a knight, but that was out of the question.

On stormy nights, I considered running away from the dresses my uncle made me wear and becoming a pirate. Whenever news of the endless war came, whenever the border disputes flared up again, I'd imagine pretending to be of common birth and apprenticing myself to the army's blacksmiths or to the messengers' guild. Anything that involved a hint of adventure and a whole lot of swords.

Anything that could help me be Splinter.

Because Splinter was the name that made my heart skip a beat and made my shoulders relax.

Splinter meant willful, like a burr in a sock. Splinter meant small but sharp and fearsome.

And maybe it wasn't as noble and heavy with history as the fancy name my parents gave me, but it didn't weigh me down. Who needs a name that fits like a coat of bricks?

Splinter was what my brother called me, before he rode off to join the battle. When I begged him to stay, he said, "We have to fight for what we believe in, Splinter. Just like our parents did."

My impossible dream was to become Splinter, become a knight like my brother, ride off to find him at the front and bring him home safe so we could be a family again.

But when my uncle became my guardian, he hid my wooden swords, forced me into dresses, and ordered me to forget.

THE CITY NEVER FORGOT ABOUT THE WAR

either.

But on the eve of the Winter's Heart Festival, I could taste excitement clean in the air. Tonight, we'd celebrate the rebirth of the year. Tonight, we'd light beacons all across the city. In the streets. On the floating docks. Across the palace battlements.

And in the princess's walled garden, because she would celebrate her twelfth birthday with a masked dance. And I was expected to be there, like a good and proper DuLac.

The party doubled as a way for the princess's parents to show off the youngest royal, second in line to the throne, who had spent the last few years in the Convent of the Peaks.

Parties were the perfect way to show our loyalty, my uncle said. And as the youngest of our noble house, the only DuLac the same age as the princess, I would behave like a member of the court, or he'd ship me off to the Fields the day after the festival. As far as my uncle was concerned, political power was the only thing that mattered in Haven. After my mother's death, the DuLacs' influence at the royal court had dwindled, and if I didn't do something about that, I'd be useless to my uncle. He'd be better off without me underfoot, and he didn't care that the only home I'd ever known was right here in this crooked old mansion.

He never asked me what I wanted.

Frankly, I didn't really care about him either.

"All those stuck-up nobles will have a fit if you show up in riding skirts."

"I know."

"Good. I'm not saying you shouldn't, but . . ." Camille, my best friend and partner in crime, looked at me critically. He wore a narrow silver band with our family crest on it on his ring finger. His family had been in service to mine for generations. He was as much a sibling to me as a servant, and I didn't want to have to miss him too. "Will it hurt terribly to just wear the dress for one night?"

I wrapped my arms across my chest and stared him down. The idea of a dress made my skin crawl. And I'd become increasingly convinced my uncle would probably send me to the convent anyway, so maybe it was worth it to go out on my own terms. "Yes."

Camille nodded. "Well, in that case, we should find you something different."

"Like?" I plucked at my compromise tunic. "It's not like we can switch clothes."

He grinned, baring his buckteeth. "I would look awful in that dress. It's far too short for me."

"I'd still look worse."

"No, you'd *feel* worse. There's a difference." He tapped one finger against his chin. "It's a good idea, though. Not the swapping clothes with me, but swapping clothes with *someone*."

"Who?"

"Anders."

I titled my head so far back my neck ached. "Are you not feeling well? Are you running a fever? My brother is practically twice as tall as I am. Unless you want me to wear his tunic as another type of dress."

"He was a giant when he left, I'll admit. But he was your age once, and it's not like you're a runt either."

It's true. Anders and I had both inherited our mother's long legs and broad shoulders. And her freckles. And, according to every tutor I ever had, her talent for utter and complete chaos. I'd always considered it a compliment. But . . . "What exactly is your point?"

"It's a masked dance, right? So mask yourself."

Camille walked to the door and peeked out into the hallway. When he was certain no one would see us, he took my hand and practically dragged me to my brother's old room.

It was all dusty inside, with motes dancing in the

afternoon sun, and endless cobwebs as a reminder of the room's loneliness. The bed was covered with a bedspread, and the walls were empty of Anders's shield and swords. The large chest at the foot of the bed held only broken toys and torn maps. Memories of the squire he once was, before he came to serve the kingdom as a knight.

After Anders left for the war three years ago, I spent so many hours in this room, pretending he would just walk back in. But he didn't. And he hasn't.

And my uncle put an end to my visits. I was not meant to fight, he said, and I should put away the wooden swords and memories of my brother and learn etiquette and languages.

"Camille, you know I'm not supposed to be here," I hissed. "I don't want to get you in trouble too."

He didn't acknowledge my words but went straight for the large wardrobe, taking an iron key from his belt to unlock the door. As son of the housekeeper, Camille had access to almost any room and any closed door in the house—save for my mother's study of course. Not even I was allowed in there. "I found this the other day. I thought you might balk at the dance, so I went looking for an alternative option." He reached in and pulled out a leather chest armor.

My breath caught. The armor looked worn and beaten, but when he tossed it in my direction, the leather still felt supple in my hands. It felt warm, almost. Like sunshine.

Camille dove back into the wardrobe and reemerged with leather shoulder guards and arm guards.

A moment later, scuffed boots that laced to the knee.

Finally, he came up for air holding the blunt dagger that complemented Anders's squire gear.

"You could wear it over your riding skirts or over pants. Your choice," he said.

I shook my head. Fear stabbed at my chest like shards of ice. "I can't wear this."

I wanted to.

Camille held out the dagger to me, hilt-first. "It's a masked dance. You're allowed."

"If my uncle finds out . . ."

"I'll help you escape if you have to." He smiled softly, sadly. I couldn't imagine being separated from him. "Living someone else's truth isn't living. For one night, you could be exactly who you want to be."

It was a brave, bold idea.

IT WAS A MISTAKE.

I'd never met Princess Adelisa, but I'd been to the walled garden before. I knew where to go. I knew to keep my hood up high, raise my shoulders to my ears, and sweep past the guards, with the invitation sticking out between my fingers. Thankfully, my uncle had been so busy preparing the city for the Winter's Heart Festival that he didn't have the time to see me off.

The leather armor that may have been comfortable for Anders chafed in awkward places. As if to remind me it wasn't made for me. Even though I wore a supple black feather mask, the moment I took off my cloak, I was convinced everyone would immediately see me for who I was, and I was not used to that.

And when all those present turned to see who had arrived, I felt utter and complete terror. As though every conversation had dropped and the musicians in the corner had put down their zithers and lutes.

They could see me. They could see I didn't fit. In more ways than one. There were no other squires there. There were noble sons, in leathers far cleaner and better kept than mine, who wore blunted daggers and the badges of prince's companion. There were noble sons in long tunics and elaborate masks, who reeked of riches and influence.

There were noble daughters in dresses that made me shiver, because they looked like prisons and promises.

And suddenly I felt like an impostor. I felt stuck between the nobility and their expectations, and there was no one—not that I knew of—no one else like me. I wanted to be Splinter. But Splinter wasn't a girl. Splinter wasn't a boy either. Splinter simply was.

I wanted to turn away, if doing so wouldn't be an unforgivable stain on Anders's armor, Camille's hard work, and my own pride.

So I did the courageous thing. I fled along one of the paths, far from the crowds.

"YOU, SQUIRE!"

I'd barely made it into the flower maze when a voice called out to me. Torn between running and turning, I stumbled. I thrust my hands forward to grasp a stone wall and keep myself from falling completely. I cleared my throat before I could find my voice. "Yes?"

I stared at my feet.

"I need help." The voice sounded annoyed, more than anything. And young—my age. Maybe not too threatening.

I balled my fists and turned around to see a masked figure on hands and knees in the sloped grass a few feet from me.

My heart slammed into my throat, distracting me from my fear. "Are you hurt?"

I rushed over.

She wore a long midnight-blue dress and sensible leather sandals that peeked out from under the hem. Her mask was slightly crooked and she quickly shoved it in place. But she didn't push herself further. "I could use a hand," she snapped.

I reached out to her, and with a soft groan, she let me pull her to her feet.

When she stood and brushed the dirt off her dress with gloved hands, she was almost my height, but I could see she favored one leg. And she *scowled*. "My crutch lies there somewhere. Find it for me." She breathed hard, and added, "Please."

A true squire wouldn't refuse, so I didn't either. But I grumbled.

With only the light of lanterns and torches to go by, it took me altogether too long to find the crutch, which had rolled down the slope. The girl in the blue dress offered only impatient noises.

Eventually my fingers glanced over a twisted wooden staff, and when I pulled it close, I could make out the support at the top. "Found it!"

"Finally."

I was briefly tempted to leave the crutch at the bottom of the slope, except I knew it would be an awful thing to do. And when I made it back to the girl, she grimaced her contrition. "I'm sorry. You were kind enough to aid me and I'm horrible."

"I . . ." I handed the crutch to her and she shifted her weight to be divided more evenly.

"It was my own fault too. I shouldn't have wandered off the path, but I couldn't stand the crowds in the main square." She looked behind her, as though they might have followed her here.

This, at least, I understood. "You don't like parties?"

"I don't like crowds."

"Me neither."

"Then why are you here?"

I shrugged. "Probably for the same reason you are."

"*Court.* That tedious gathering of greedy nobles who only care about having the loudest voice, the most coin, the biggest influence on the queen. Their gossip is sharper than their blades, but both are pointless."

I bit back a smile at the sheer disdain in her voice.

We looked at each other. I nodded at the flower maze just past her. In the near dark, it looked like a mysterious place, full of shadows and adventures. "If parties are a way to show loyalty, like my uncle claims, we only need to be seen here, right? We have the whole evening. We could walk the maze and stay away from the main square."

The girl's eyes were curious and calculating behind her mask, but her shoulders relaxed a bit. With her free hand, she pushed a lock of unruly brown hair behind one ear. She couldn't be much older than me, though she wore nobility far more comfortably. "What's your name?"

I licked my lips. I saw the opportunity, and I caught it with both hands. "Splinter."

She furrowed her brow. "That can't be a real name."

It was a name I had been given. A name I had chosen. Didn't that make it real? "Then what is yours?"

She hesitated too. "Ash."

"Of course *that* is a real name."

"It's the only one you'll get." She smiled, and it brightened up her whole face. "Lead the way, Splinter."

ASH AND I CIRCLED THROUGH THE FLOWER

maze twice, while the shadows lengthened and the evening grew darker. We would soon reach the point of midnight and the lighting of the beacons. I led the way the first time, and Ash immediately memorized it.

"I like mazes," she said, when I commented on it. "They're problems with solutions."

"I wish every problem had a solution as easy as this," I said, before I could stop myself.

Ash glanced at me sideways, and took a long time before she spoke. "Not everything that's worthwhile is easy."

I thought about walking into the party dressed as the person I wanted to be. I thought about introducing myself as Splinter. I thought about going back to being the wretched girl who punched the prince. And maybe it was the mask that gave me courage, because I added, "But some things are so impossibly hard they break you from the inside."

Ash nodded. "True."

She didn't say anything else about it. We talked about other things. She came from the mountains and hadn't been to the city in years; I'd never been anywhere but the city. She didn't get along well with her older brother; I missed mine. Occasionally, music from the main square drifted our way.

Eventually, she asked the questions I dreaded most. "Who are you squired to? Who are your parents?"

My heart somersaulted and my hands grew cold. I didn't have an answer to either of those questions. I wasn't a squire. And my family name would immediately turn me into the girl I wasn't either.

I drew breath to speak, to say—I don't know what I wanted to say—when a scream tore through the garden. Ash and I turned at the same time.

I was the first to spot the two in the meadow across the maze. A lanky guard and a girl a little older than us who was trying her best to get away from him. Her face looked blotched and tear-stained. And I felt fire course through me. All I could think of was that time I punched the crown prince, because he was also bullying a girl. So I ran.

Running away from crowds is easy. Running toward bullies is easier.

"Not at *my* party," Ash muttered under her breath behind me. She ran too. With her crutch making big strides, she could almost keep pace with me. When I reached the guard and the girl, two things happened at once.

The girl stamped on the guard's foot and I lunged for his arm, trying to pull him off balance.

He hadn't seen me coming, and when I grabbed him, he yelped and reacted, using hand-to-hand skills I definitely didn't have. He swung me around the girl and I went down. I scrambled back to my feet immediately.

"Let her go."

The guard snarled.

Ash slammed the butt of her crutch against the guardsman's knee, making him lose his grasp on the girl. In the process, Ash stumbled on the uneven surfaces. The guard flinched and turned toward me, making him the perfect target.

I punched him in the nose.

I felt something crunch beneath my fist.

He yowled.

My knuckles throbbed.

And the girl took the opportunity to dash away from us.

The guard turned toward me and Ash, red with rage. Without really thinking about it, I stepped in front of Ash, fists held high in case I needed to punch him again.

The guard pulled his arm back to lash out at me when Ash's voice rang through the garden. *"Don't you dare."*

He froze.

Other hands swam into my vision, and two guards dragged the attacker away. A third clamped a hand around my upper arm and tried to pull me from Ash. When I resisted, he pushed my mask aside and immediately recognized me. "You."

In all fairness to the guards, I wasn't just the person who punched the prince. I was the person who gave the prince a black eye and didn't regret it.

I scowled at the guard. "I didn't do anything. Let me go."

I glanced around. The girl who had been attacked stood near the entrance to the meadow. She was frantically gesturing and explaining things to a man in a captain's tunic. But the captain only had eyes for me.

How was I going to explain this to my uncle?

Then I realized the captain was looking slightly past me, at Ash.

Ash, who had scrambled to her feet.

Ash, who had taken off her mask and her gloves and who was staring at me.

Ash, who looked the spitting image of the crown prince, but with kinder eyes. Ash, who wore the royal crest on her finger.

My party.

I stared at her. Everything clicked together in my mind.

"You're the one who punched my brother," she said.

"You're the *princess*."

We spoke at nearly the same time and our words hung in the air between us.

Belatedly, I realized I should curtsy—or bow.

Ash—*Princess Adelisa*—didn't seem much bothered, though. She looked past me at the guard who was still holding on to my arm. With her shoulders squared and her head held high, she was every inch royalty. "You heard what happened. Let . . ." She hesitated and blinked. "Let *go*. Let us both go."

"But, Highness—"

"No."

"We have to take statements. This girl has a history of violence."

I flinched in his grasp.

Ash narrowed her eyes. "Leave. Now."

Behind us, the captain called an order, amusement clear in his tone.

The guard let go of me, and they all pulled back, taking the guard with the broken nose with them. Leaving Ash and me alone in the quiet garden.

I shook my arm out and winced. I could still feel the impression of the guard's fingers. "I wish I could be that strong." My voice wavered.

"Apparently you looked like a threat to them."

I pulled my cloak closer around my shoulders and purposefully didn't meet her gaze. "They'd get along well with my uncle."

"The crown prince too, probably." Her voice trembled slightly.

When I peeked up at her, she indicated with her head. "Come on. Let's walk."

WE FOUND A STONE WALL IN THE FLOWER

maze, not far from where we had stumbled onto the guard and the girl. She sat down, royally, and motioned for me to sit too, so she could observe me.

"You should read the stories my brother writes of you. What *is* your name?"

I bit my lip and stared at her. She was a bit disheveled from the scuffle, but her eyes still sparkled, and the way she almost-but-not-quite smiled almost made me forget about the chafing of Anders's armor. She didn't laugh or scoff at me.

Then she tapped her foot impatiently. "Are you ignoring me?"

I cleared my throat. "No, my lady."

"Whose armor is this?"

"My brother's."

"He's off to the northern front?"

"Yes."

"And you're not a real squire."

"No."

"But you want to be?"

I hesitated for only the briefest of moments. It happened, of course, that boys were assumed to be girls and took the long way to their swords. But even though I loved Camille for bringing me Anders's armor, that wasn't me. I didn't want to live that lie either. "I'm not a boy."

"But you're not a girl either."

The simple statement took my breath away.

"I'm not as ignorant as people think I am," she continued. "They see my crutch and think I know nothing about the world." She shrugged. "They're not completely wrong. I don't know enough about the world. Not by half. But I see more than most people want me to."

I'd already noticed that.

"Court is going to hate you," I blurted out. That was the one thing I had learned from my uncle. The people whose only worth lies in power don't take kindly to the people who question too much, demand too much, try to be better.

Her crooked smile was grim. "I know."

She glanced at me and her smile turned warmer. And in that smile, I saw all that she was. Royal and kind, impatient words and fierce determination and so much trouble. I saw the same glint that was in Camille's eyes whenever he bended and twisted the city's expectations. "I could use a friend at court," she said.

I shook my head and plucked at the leather armor. "This was a midwinter night's dream. When word gets out about what happened here, my uncle will have me on a cart to the convent before sundown tomorrow."

"But you won't be happy there."

It was a statement, and I couldn't deny it. I wouldn't be. I'd rather run away and become a sailor. A farrier. A runner in the army. I'd lose my home regardless. Maybe I could build a new one somewhere. Away from my uncle. Away from his expectations.

Away from Anders and Camille.

The silence fell heavy between us.

Then Ash—Princess Adelisa—narrowed her eyes. "You didn't answer my question. Do you want to be a squire?"

I rubbed my swollen knuckles ruefully. "I want nothing more. I want to be able to fight for what I believe in."

"And what do you believe in?"

No one had ever asked me that question, and I hesitated. "I believe in my brother. I believe in putting an end to the war." I pushed on. "I believe that I should be allowed to be who I want to be—who I *am*."

"Those aren't small dreams."

"Not everything worthwhile is easy," I said. I spoke the words with a smile, even though they hurt.

"Do you believe in me?"

I looked at her and felt the stirrings of something. Like fireflies in my stomach and the sea breeze on my face. Like the deep inhale before the beacons of the Winter's Heart Festival were lit. Even if we went back to normal the next day, even if I ended up at (and would escape from) a convent two days later, she had accepted me. She'd *seen* me. "Yes."

She nodded as if that settled something. "Good." She pulled off one of her rings and casually held it out to me. "You'll be my squire, then."

Oh.

"It isn't just a simple solution because your uncle can't say no to me," she continued. "I *want* you to be my squire."

Again she left me breathless.

All I could manage was, "That isn't how things are normally done. Princesses don't *have* squires."

She shrugged. She held my dream in the palm of her hand. "Princesses don't normally punch guardsmen either."

"You like to make things difficult for yourself," I suggested. It sounded so much like my uncle that it left a bad taste in my mouth, but my mind was twisting and turning and tumbling over itself.

She grinned, baring her teeth. "I like to make things difficult for the people who deserve it." She reached for my hand and dropped the ring in my palm and dropped the mask that hid her loneliness. "I want to be able to fight for what I believe in too. I don't want to be alone here. Life at court terrifies me. Life in the city terrifies me. And I can't promise you you'll ever be allowed to be a knight, but you'll be my companion. I promise you'll never have to be anyone you're not."

I made a split-second decision. She needed me as much as I needed her.

I curled my fingers around the ring and with my

other hand reached for where my brother's dagger hung. Where my sword would one day be. "I'll be your squire."

She stilled. She looked so relieved. "You will?"

I took her hand. "I promise on the broken nose of your guard. I'll be your squire and your friend . . . Ash."

"Thank you"—she looked at me with that one unanswered question in her eyes and on her lips, but before she could ask it, I shook my head, and after a desperately long silence, she nodded—"Splinter."

A cheer from the garden distracted us from our moment. On the castle's battlements, the first beacons had been lit. I slipped the ring on my finger and it felt as if the leather armor fitted a bit more comfortably. "I can't wait for our brothers to find out," I said.

I could feel her grin. "I think we'll make a fearsome team."

And while the light spread throughout the city, beacon by beacon, lantern by lantern, Ash took my hand in hers. We sat on the low wall, the princess and the squire, leaning against each other ever so slightly. And in front of us, the New Year began.

Menudo Fan Club

BY AIDA SALAZAR

I

I don't like menudo
not the stew my ámi cooks on Sunday mornings
because it smells with a hint of poop
nor Menudo, the band,
who's played over and over and over
on the radio.

Same difference.

Everyone in the neighborhood
is bananas for those
five boys from Puerto Rico.
*   The girls on TV especially.*
They faint and fall

all
　　　　over
themselves
　　like fumigated roaches.

It's ridiculous.
I don't know why
they're such a big deal.

Worse part is, Camila likes them too!
All of a sudden, my friend,
the girl who used to lend me
　　one of her skates
　　so we could ride
　　one-legged
　　down the block
is too busy for skating
and more interested in guys with long hair
and stretchy spandex pants
who dance the cheesiest choreography
to the crappiest songs.

I just don't get it.

II

Camila lives in the house
with a jacaranda tree out front
a tree that blooms
each year in the spring
and whose fallen purple trumpet flowers
we'd run to pounce on
just to hear them pop and smack
beneath our jelly shoes.

My house is exactly
ten houses from hers
and it's been about
ten months since
she's really been my friend.

Her Catholic school broke up
our friendship like a cookie
    down the middle.
It's not like she hated me or anything.
Things just got weird
after we started sixth grade
no matter that we were
only ten houses away.

I blame it on her scholarship.
She'd complain,
The nuns are going to
kick me out if I don't keep up!
I tried to help her because
my public middle school was a cinch for me
but it was *hard stuff, Catholic school.*

Instead of studying, we'd go out
   on her front lawn
            lay on our backs and tangle
   our legs together and giggle
at how the night swallowed the sunset.
   I felt light and breathless
   to lay there next to her
   grass tickling our arms
and pretend the tiny moving lights
            from the flying airplanes above
                  were stars.

I had a feeling that maybe
I was being too distracting
and so, I just stopped coming over
I didn't want to get
   in her way.

Now the summer's here
and we're officially seventh graders
and I'm walking up the block
toward the jacaranda tree
my heart doing somersaults
because she left a note
with my brother Mateo
while I was in the shower.
It's an invitation for me to join
    "THE MENUDO FAN CLUB"
she wrote in big bubble letters
which brought back the stars for me
so fast, I couldn't say no
and I am swallowing my disgust
like a big fat vitamin
mostly because I miss Camila
and would really like
to see her
again.

III

As I go down the wide driveway
my mouth sways into a smile
to remember the roller derby

we set up in her carport
only a couple of years ago
and how the song "Xanadu"
by Olivia Newton-John
sometimes played on the boom box
            while we
        rolled,   skated,
and biked   in a circle
            for hours
                until our mothers
        called us in
pa' comer.

My eyes blink as they adjust
from the shining sun as I step
        into her father's toolshed
        by the carport.
There are a few girls
one I sorta know and some I don't
setting out Twinkies on a plate
or standing   Menudo albums
                upright
                on a table.
The walls of the shed
are covered by posters

of the skinny Menudo boys:
Charlie, René, Johnny,
Miguel, Ricky.
Yuck.

It could be a record store
dedicated to Menudo
but it smells like rusty metal
and dried mowed grass.

IV

Hey, D! Ven, ven. Come in.
I'm so glad you got my note.
We so needed a fifth girl
to complete the fan club.
We're about to start.

I almost don't recognize Camila
her face has grown
into a different kind of blossom
strange and long and sorta grown up.
Missing was the sun-kissed brown
that drenched her skin
in the forever-hot LA weather

and the streams of dried salty
sweat that always marked
her face from the temples
down her cheeks.

Suddenly, I realize
she's wearing makeup.

Lots of it.

> *Glimmering soft blue eye shadow*
> *navy-blue eyeliner*
> *mascara so thick it makes her lashes*
> *look like spokes on a wheel*
> *and lipstick so bright pink*
> *it could glow in the dark.*

Her neon yellow tank top
is really filled in
>   *right on the chest*
and I can't help but stare
>   *and wonder*
how she grew those so quickly?

I look down at my own chest
still cardboard flat
and bite my lower lip

for just a second until
I see that another girl here
is in the cardboard society
and then I take a big breath
with my makeup-less mouth.

Camila is smooth and smiles as she
takes a nine-inch record from its case
careful not to scratch the vinyl
then places it on the player
turns on the machine
watches the disc spin
and lays the needle
on the record
right
on
the
edge.

Ven claridad, llega ya,
amanece de una vez, claridad . . .

Cheesy sounds crackle
from the player into the air.
I feel slightly nauseous at first.
These lyrics are the pits

but to see Camila's whole body
    sweep into that song
        in a whirl of happiness
    makes me recalibrate
and I feel a flutter
    in my tripas instead.

She looks shiny
    dancing against
        the bright sunlight
that comes into our Menudo shed.
I wish I could dance with her
    eyes half-closed
our hands in a clasp.

But now I'm not sure it's a feeling
I'm supposed to have for her
so I just continue to look and listen
to Menudo's girl-like voices
sing in harmony about
the wish for clarity to come
and take over the darkness.

V

As president of Carmelita Street's
one and only Menudo Fan Club
I'd like to welcome you.
    Camila semi-sings over the music.
Our first order of business
is for us to claim
our favorite boy.

Girl squeals ring out so high
they make the tin roof vibrate.
I claim Miguel!
    Oooh, mine is René!
¡Johnny es mio!

Camila zeroes in on her boy,
I call Charlie! He's sooo chulo!
And then she turns to me.
What about you, D?

I freeze.

All of the girls
inspect me for clues.
I know they're reading my eyes
as they bounce up with mine to the biggest poster

of the five boys looking seductively
at the camera with their feathered hair
wearing different-colored spandex
and sleeveless jumpsuits.

I—I—I . . . don't know, *I stutter.*

Well, you've got to choose one
to claim your membership to the club.
Camila's sweet face bends into a sudden frown.

I want to say,
> *You, Camila.*
> *You're my person.*
> *You're the one I want to listen to sing,*
> *the one whose music I want to dance to*
> *the one I want to dance with*
> *the one whose poster I want to put up.*
> *You, Camila, even with the makeup*
> *and the filled-in tank top*
> *still like the old Camila*
> *with tangled legs on the grass*
> *and watching stars*
> *the old Camila skating*
> *to disco derby music*
> *and laughing out loud*

and twirling
and twirling
and twirling
in jelly shoes
beneath the jacaranda
blooms about to fall
across the yard
and spill their purple
color all over Carmelita Street
like your laughter.

But I am silent,
look up into that poster
too embarrassed
by my own feelings
of being a girl
liking another girl.

Come on, D! Just pick a boy
or I'll have to give you one.

I finally move my eyes down
from the poster and they
land as delicately as they can
on Camila.
I hope that is enough of an answer.

I hope the Menudo fan clubbers
can see that I've chosen.

Ay, fine. I'm giving you Ricky.
Don't worry, D, you'll like him
in no time at all.

I force a smile
certain and sad that Camila
doesn't feel for me
like I do for her.
I bury my tugging
heart back into my body
as the tune about claridad ends
and another one begins.

Stacy's Mom

BY NICOLE MELLEBY

ABIGAIL WAS FIVE the first time she fell in love. It coincided with a tumble off her bike and a skinned knee.

The fall happened right in front of Stacy Mackenzie's house. This is important to know, because Stacy's mom worked at home, and she saw the entire incident from her living room window. She was outside the front door before Stacy even dismounted her own bike, and as she fussed over Abigail, Abigail's mind took the time to think, *Stacy's mom has the softest hair*, regardless of the pain.

Mrs. Mackenzie blew softly on Abigail's scraped knee. Abigail sat on top of the bathroom sink, watching closely as Mrs. Mackenzie wiped at the blood and the dirt, enjoying the soft *shh* Mrs. Mackenzie gave her when she winced at the pain of the alcohol swab.

Stacy made funny faces from the doorway while her

mom pressed gently on the edges of the bandage she applied to Abigail's knee. Abigail didn't laugh. She was too caught up thinking, *Stacy's mom has the prettiest eyes,* and wishing her scrape was bigger, would take more time to fix up, would keep Mrs. Mackenzie's focus on her longer.

For the entire week after the event, Abigail toyed with the peeling corners of the Band-Aid, refusing to change it even when the edges frayed and turned brown with dirt.

Infection be damned, Abigail was in love.

She was almost disappointed when the wound healed.

IT IS ALSO IMPORTANT TO KNOW THAT

Abigail attended a very small Catholic middle school. What happens at a very small Catholic middle school is that, on Friday after dismissal, students will cluster together and go to their friends' houses and the movies and the ice-skating rink after kicking off their uncomfortable pleated skirts and starchy button-up shirts. If something happens at a friend's house, or the movies, or the ice-skating rink, it becomes a game of wildfire, spreading from cell phone to cell phone to cell phone—until it reaches *everybody.*

If anything happens on a Friday night, the entire

small Catholic school student body will know about it come Monday.

This is important, because Abigail had been one of those students on a Monday morning, gasping in shock when she and Stacy heard that Lindsey tripped over her own skates and fell on the ice, her skirt no match for the way she slid across it, revealing her underwear to Lucas (who took photos). Abigail had been one of those students who stifled laughter into their hands during Miss Santos's class when they found out that Amara's mom caught her and Leo kissing in the back row of the movie theater. Abigail had been one of those students who gossiped and wondered out loud about Manuel when he came out as trans to Sofia in the privacy of Sofia's basement.

However, from first all the way to sixth grade, Abigail had not yet been the student who was talked about on Monday.

This was perhaps the most important fact of all.

IT HAPPENED AT 3:36 ON A FRIDAY, THE day of the week during which these things always did.

At 3:21, Stacy's mom was microwaving pizza bagels while Stacy, Lindsey, and Maya were in Stacy's room trading their uniform skirts for sweatpants. Abigail was in the kitchen, sitting with Mrs. Mackenzie, waiting to bring the nearly heated snacks upstairs. "I watched that show on Netflix you told me to," Abigail said. "It was really good."

"I knew you'd like it," Stacy's mom said, smiling just for Abigail. (It *had* to be just for Abigail, since no one else was around, and no one else had been told to watch the show in the first place. Abigail didn't even tell Stacy she was going to watch it—she wanted to keep it for herself.)

(Just like she kept the leftovers that Mrs. Mackenzie always sent her home with to herself, the rest of her family be damned.)

(And just like she had once kept a dirty, dingy Band-Aid under her bed back when she was five, until her mom did a deep clean of her bedroom and tossed it.)

Abigail must have been smiling, cheeks flushed and warmed as she carried those pizza bagels into Stacy's bedroom.

Because, at 3:35, Maya rolled her eyes, saying, "What *is* it with you with Stacy's mom?"

Stacy's eyes narrowed. Lindsey audibly gasped.

"What?" Maya said, shrugging. "You all know how she is around Mrs. Mackenzie."

All three of them turned to stare at Abigail. The plate in her hands felt too warm and she was suddenly too hot and she needed a place to sit down.

"I—I don't," Abigail stuttered. "I mean, I'm not . . ."

"Not *what*?" Stacy asked.

"I just think your mom's really pretty."

ABIGAIL DIDN'T TEXT ANYONE SATURDAY

(no one seemed interested in texting her, either), but she had a feeling in her stomach, much like the moment before hitting the ground after falling off a bike, that everyone was texting *about* her.

She tried to tell herself she was being ridiculous, as she hovered in the living room while her mom graded papers, just in case Stacy's mom called, just in case Stacy's mom *knew*, and for some reason decided to tattle.

But Stacy's mom never called, and apparently Stacy and Maya had gone to Starbucks, to the mall, to Timoney's Pizzeria, to Stacy's house. Which wasn't unusual on a Saturday afternoon, but the silence on Abigail's phone was. She had never not been invited before.

Thanks to social media, Abigail was able to watch every single thing they did without her, knowing that the way her heart started racing when she caught sight of Stacy's mom in the background of one of those photos was the reason they avoided her.

ON SUNDAY, ABIGAIL'S MOM BROUGHT HER
to church like always. It was cloudy; the stained glass
along the walls and ceiling dimmed, the dark wood of
the pews draped in shadows. It made for a fitting background, as Abigail wondered if she should even be allowed inside.

She avoided searching for Stacy and her family, even
though she had spent six years' worth of Sundays keeping
an eye out for her best friend. Abigail and Stacy would
make faces at each other as the priest spoke. Abigail would
watch as Stacy's mom sang along with all the psalms.

Abigail didn't make eye contact with anyone now, except for a quick stolen glance up at Jesus, hanging on a
cross above the altar. He stared right back at her, crown
of thorns on his head and all.

The only thing Abigail could think was, *Please stop
looking at me like that.*

THAT IS HOW, EVEN THOUGH SHE HAD
eluded it for six entire school years, Abigail became the
student everyone was talking about come Monday.

And it wasn't just all in Abigail's head, if the whispers

and hand-covered laughter and glances in her direction were any indication.

They *were* an indication. So was the fact that when Abigail went out of her way, past her homeroom, to find Stacy at her locker, Stacy blew her off with a quick "I have to go. I need to get my homework back from Maya."

"I didn't mean to upset you, Stacy."

"You didn't upset me," Stacy said, closing her locker. "It's my mom and it's awkward and you never even told me you were gay."

Stacy didn't wait for Abigail to respond. Which was fine, because Abigail didn't know how to respond to that anyway.

She kept her head down as she quickly made her way to her seat in homeroom, ignoring the way Lucas coughed something under his breath at her that made Leo laugh, ignoring the heat on the back of her neck she hoped no one could notice under her hair, and ignoring the way holding back tears made her nose burn. Miss Santos shushed them from the front of the room, but all Abigail could think about was how many Mondays she had spent whispering about someone else, laughing about someone else, gossiping about someone else.

She felt guilty for that. Just like she felt guilty for going to church and felt guilty for crushing on Stacy's mom in the first place.

(Would this have happened if her crush was on Stacy's dad, or Maya's brother, or the boys from One Direction?)

It didn't matter. Abigail didn't have crushes on men like Stacy's dad or boys like Maya's brother or male celebrities like One Direction. She had crushes on women with dark wavy hair that tickled against her cheeks after a spill off her bike, and pretty eyes and laugh lines.

She had crushes on women like Mrs. Mackenzie, and God help her, her body was still betraying her with fluttery feelings in her stomach just thinking about Stacy's mom.

"They'll move on. You'll be old news by Friday, the latest."

The voice interrupted Abigail's inner monologue before she could fully shame herself right onto the floor.

(Pay attention. This part's important.)

It was Lindsey, sitting in front of her, turning around in her chair. She leaned even closer to Abigail to whisper, "You're right, though. Stacy's mom is really pretty."

Abigail thought she was being made fun of. (Again.)

But that's when Lindsey added, "But *I* think Miss Santos is really, really pretty, too."

Sylvie & Jenna

BY ASHLEY HERRING BLAKE

THE NEW GIRL is staring at me.

Or, I guess you could argue that I'm staring at her, but she's staring right back. This wouldn't be a big deal—a new student walks into an eighth-grade English classroom in the middle of October with shiny dark red hair down to her waist, black-framed glasses, and purple-and-white-striped leggings under a gray shift dress, the girl is going to get looked at.

Only one problem. After Ms. Amalfi introduces her as "Jenna from Seattle, let's give her a warm welcome," after the girl sits at a desk next to mine, I can't seem to *stop* staring. She, of course, has moved on from me, busying herself with getting out a notebook (bright green with cartoon cats all over it) and a pen (gel, purple ink), but here I am, gaping like a fish, my stomach fizzing like I just downed a two-liter of Mountain Dew.

"Okay, everyone," Ms. Amalfi says, clapping her brown hands and then tucking her dark hair behind her ears, "as I mentioned before, we're starting our poetry unit, and we're going to kick it off with everyone's favorite recluse, Emily Dickinson. . . ."

My teacher's voice fades into the back of my mind, free verse and hope and feathers and all that. Meanwhile, my eyes have grown their own brain cells and seem to be permanently stuck to the side of Jenna's face. She's got freckles on her nose, brown eyes. There's something familiar about her, but as my moms own our small Oregon town's only bakery, I see hundreds of people a week when I help out after school and during the summer, tourists and locals alike. If Jenna just moved to Landry Falls, chances are she's already been to Sugar & Star and feasted on Mimi's nationally famous salted-caramel scones, and I was too caught up in a wave of pastry-crazed customers to really take her in.

Now, though, in the warm light of Ms. Amalfi's "Lamps only, please!" classroom, I feel like I may never look at anyone else ever again.

Until, without any warning whatsoever, Jenna turns to look right back at me. From across the room, while she stood with our teacher, no big deal, but right here, in the second-to-last row of desks, not even an arm's length between us, it feels totally different. She's close.

So close I can see that she's got a few more freckles on the right side of her face than on the left. Her eyebrows lift in question—beautiful eyebrows, by the way, thick and straight and dark and—

I look away fast, my cheeks warm. Marnie, my best friend for the last two years, who's currently sitting behind me and watching me make a complete fool of myself, kicks my chair's legs, a not-so-subtle *slow your roll, Sylvie.*

I need to slow so many rolls lately. But I can't help it. Ever since this past summer, when I finally came out as gay to my moms, to Marnie, to everyone in our whole town, in fact, and to very little fanfare and lots of *good for you*s, I've been romance-addled, lovestruck, starry-eyed, whatever you want to call it. I can't seem to get enough of all the new Netflix rom-coms or Mom's quirky romance novels that she keeps organized by color on a shelf in our living room. Her favorite author, Evelyn Bly, writes a lot of queer romance; I've read all six of her books at least three times now.

Of course by *read,* I mean devoured under my covers with my phone's flashlight long after my moms think I'm in bed, because Mom has said more than once that I can't read Evelyn's books until I'm at least thirty-five, but whatever. Evelyn's books are life. All those *glances* between the characters. All that *looking* and *longing* and hands brushing as they pass the salt and that first kiss. I mean, sure, Evelyn's characters usually end up doing a lot more than kissing, but it's nothing my moms didn't already tell me about when we had the big S-E-X talk a few years ago. Evelyn's stories are *romantic*. They're about *love*, not just making out.

Don't get me wrong, making out sounds pretty cool too. But really, I just want to hold hands with someone at the movies. Or maybe while walking down the sidewalk in town, all out in the open and proud. I've never really had a crush on anyone. I tried to get into boys when everyone around me was starting to blush and giggle in the fifth grade, but I never felt anything other than a slight distaste at all the burping going on at the boys' lunch table.

Plus, I was too busy hiding under rocks in elementary school, trying to escape the nickname She-Who-Shall-Not-Be-Named pinned on me in the second grade when I accidentally wet my pants during the holiday chorus program we performed for the parents. Right there in the front row, my bright green leggings turned a darker shade as pee leaked down my legs, in front of what might as well have been the entire town, while everyone around me sang about a winter wonderland. In my defense, nerves make my bladder all twitchy and my brain all forgetful, which is why I hadn't gone to the bathroom before the concert. And with Evil Incarnate, Jennifer McCaffrey, singing her heart out right next to me, things were bound to go south.

Soggy Sylvie.

That's what she called me, after the concert was over and we all met back in Mr. Wheeler's music room to turn in our reindeer props and jingle bells.

"Oh my God, Soggy Sylvie," Jennifer had said, the bell in her hand ringing as she covered her mouth in horror. "Need a diaper?"

I'd stood there, mortified, hoping against all hope that the wet down my legs wasn't *that* noticeable, which of course it was and of course my life was officially over.

Mimi and Mom let me stay home from school the next day, but after that, I had to dry it up and face the horror that was the rest of elementary school with *Soggy Sylvie* latched onto my shoulders like a sloth. Looking back, I'm sure most people forgot about it after a couple of weeks. Jennifer never called me that name ever again, and I'd go weeks without thinking about it. But then someone would bring it up, like during gym or when our teacher directed us to make sure and use the restroom before getting on the bus for a field trip. Some jerk like Rye Fielding or Katie Crumbley would eye me and say, "Hear that, Soggy Bottom? Make sure and use the potty, okay?" and everyone would snicker and look at me and my face would ignite and I'd wish the rest of my body would catch fire too.

Off and on it went. By fifth grade, I still carried the name around like a soggy backpack. Every now and then, I'd catch Jennifer looking at me, her happy and beautiful friends all around her, like she wanted to rub in the fact that she was perfect and I was a weirdo.

But then, Jennifer's family moved away the summer after fifth grade. Once middle school started in the fall, it was like *poof!* Fresh start. No more Soggy Sylvie. Everyone forgot about it. More importantly, no one *cared*. It was second grade, after all, and now we were big-time middle schoolers, way too mature for mean nicknames. At least that's what I told myself. Really, I think everyone was just scared out of their minds to start Landry Falls Middle, with all the rotating classes and five different teachers and *eighth graders* as tall as oak trees, and we had to band together to survive. I started actually talking to people in class and at lunch, making friends. I joined the band and started playing the marimba, which is like a xylophone but with wooden bars rather than metal ones, and rubber mallets. What's more, I'm really good at percussion stuff and can pick out almost any song on my soprano marimba at home. Halfway through sixth grade, Marnie showed up, and it was like I got a best friend overnight. We loved the same things—she played the marimba too, which, come on, it's fate!—and she had a hyphenated name just like me, because she had two dads. Tim and Barron became fast friends with Mom and Mimi, and now the six of us are together almost every weekend, cooking and watching movies at our house or Marnie's.

Through all of this, I also figured out that I didn't like boys *that way* at all. When Marnie started talking about Jake Ling in the seventh grade, lying on my bed with her eyes all glazed over and babbling on and on about how cute he was and how she wondered if he had nice breath and *oh my God, Sylvie, can you imagine touching a boy's tongue with your tongue,* I had to admit that no, no, I could not imagine it.

But I could imagine it with a girl.

It started out with small things. Like realizing that I paid way more attention to Black Widow and Captain Marvel than I did Thor or Iron Man or Captain America. Like, *way* more. Then, the summer after seventh grade, I kept watching the teenage girls at the pool. Which got a little confusing, because, yeah, they were older and pretty and in high school, so of course I was going to look at them and wonder if I'd be that cool in a few years, or that confident with the curves that were already starting to fill out my bathing suit. Of course I wanted to be just like them.

But then Marnie would slap my arm and nod toward

one of the teenage boys. She'd blush and giggle at his *chest hair.* She'd call him cute and dreamy, and I . . . well, my eyes would drift over to one of the girls. She was probably in ninth grade. Not that much older than us. She was Black and had a halo of curls around her head. Her eyes were dark and her lips were glossy pink and she had on this one-piece with a cutout in the side, her brown hip gleaming in the sun. When she laughed, dimples pressed into her cheeks.

Cute. Dreamy.

And then I knew. I liked girls. It took me a few days to wrap my head around it. It wasn't like I was a stranger to being queer—my moms were queer, obviously, and so were Marnie's dads. And they had a lot of queer friends around town. Still, I'd never thought about what I was until recently, until everyone around me was getting all wild about *going together* and who was texting whom and school dances and I couldn't fit myself into that romantic space like Marnie could, like most of the girls in my grade could. That *boy* space.

But . . . a *girl* space. I slid right into it. Once I thought it—*I like girls*—everything clicked. I felt right, relieved, happy even. My moms were ecstatic, even though Mimi kept going on and on about how sexuality was fluid and it was okay if one day I realized I liked boys too, or nonbinary people, or anyone, but still she couldn't get the smile off her face. At our next cookout with Marnie and her dads, they even made me a rainbow cake and strung up rainbow streamers in our living room and bought rainbow party hats. I had an actual coming-out party and it was awesome. It was way more than most kids get and I'll never forget it.

A few months later, romance and love are all I can think about. Soft smiles. Running into each other around town. Holding hands. Kissing. Oh my God, *kissing*. But while all that dominates my newly out brain, it's all a dream. Unreal. There's no one girl I'm crushing on. No one face I imagine when I think about my first kiss. I don't like anyone especially. I just like the idea of liking someone.

Except now, my eyes wander back over to Jenna. Red hair. God, I love red hair. I mean, who doesn't? It looks like it might be dyed, but who cares? It's red. Like a sunset. Like fire. J . . . E . . . N . . . N . . . A. Even her name rolls off the tongue like a poem.

My chair jolts again—Marnie kicking its metal legs.

"Cool down, girl," she says, leaning over her desk to whisper close to my ear.

I turn away from Jenna and talk over my other shoulder. "I am."

"You're drooling."

"Am not."

Marnie makes a panting noise, like a dog in heat, and sticks out her tongue, follow by a whispered, "Say something to her."

"Like what?"

"Like, 'Hey, want to get married and live HEA?'"

I roll my eyes, even though my brain sort of yells out a silent whoop.

"Just, 'Hey, my name's Sylvie,'" Marnie says.

"Just like that?"

"Yeah, just like that."

I turn back to face the front of the room. Ms. Amalfi has put on a video about Dickinson's early life and flicked off the lamp on her desk. Perfect for a little romantic recon.

I breathe in. Out. In again. I can do this.

I turn in my chair so my legs face Jenna. Then I lean toward her, just a little. She's got her elbows propped on her desk, her chin in her hands. Adorable. Except she's not clueing in to my leaning. Hasn't noticed me at all.

I lean a little farther.

Behind me I hear Marnie say something that sounds suspiciously like *oh my God, it's like watching a car accident in slo-mo,* but I ignore her. I got this.

"Hi," I whisper.

Jenna doesn't move.

I clear my throat. "Um, hi."

Finally, a twitch. Behind her glasses, her eyes flick to me, but her head stays put.

"Hi?" I say one more time, and it comes out sounding like a question. My confidence shimmers like a shadow in the sun.

Still, it works. She turns her head toward me, curiosity in those perfect brows. The video ends and Ms. Amalfi turns on her lamp again, rambles about reading poems 16, 42, 153, and blah, blah, blah for homework. The bell rings and the class bursts into motion. It's now or never.

"Um, hi. I'm Sylvie."

Now Jenna's brows lift. Kids swarm around us, and I feel Marnie come up on the other side of my desk.

Jenna's gaze is still on mine. Locked. This might be a perfect moment. But then something that looks sort of like sadness spills into her eyes and she looks away, down at her notebook as she pulls it to her chest. "Yeah," she says softly. "I know."

Then she slings her messenger bag over one shoulder and hurries out of the room, head down, shoulders hunched, and my perfect moment goes *poof*.

"'I KNOW'? WHAT DOES THAT EVEN MEAN?"

It's after school and Marnie and I are sitting at a table in Sugar & Star working on homework. I've got a backlog of reading to do for English, in addition to all those poems I need to read, but I can't focus on any of it because my brain is buzzing with Jenna's proclamation.

I know.

"She probably just means that she's heard of you," Marnie says. She sticks out her tongue while penciling in her notebook about x and y and quadratic something or other.

"But how?" I'm not exactly a model student. I'm not terrible, I'm just . . . there. Solid Bs, some As, zoning out in algebra almost daily.

"It's a small town, Syl."

"Yeah. Yeah, you're right. Maybe her parents came in here and met my moms or something."

"Exactly."

"Right."

I go back to reading-slash-brooding, and Marnie keeps scribbling next to me. We settle in, that nice quiet between two friends, the kind of quiet I know Marnie loves. She's awesome, has my back no matter what, but she's an introvert, and sometimes all my babbling wears her out. What can I say? You'd talk your best friend's ear off too if you'd spent half of elementary school in friendless isolation.

Okay, that might be a tad dramatic, but still. Marnie is my BFF and therefore must receive all of my thoughts, rambling or otherwise.

"Except," I say, and Marnie groans. The bell over the door dings as more customers pour in. "She said it like she was . . . sad about it. Like *knowing* made her sad."

"So why don't you go ask her?" Marnie says.

"What?"

Marnie points her pencil toward the line at the pastry case and there, *right there,* is Jenna. She's wearing the same clothes she wore at school—of course she is, it's only been like thirty minutes since we got out—and has her bag over her shoulder. She's standing with a woman I guess is her mom. They're quiet, both of their shoulders sort of rounded, like they're carrying something heavy. The woman hooks an arm around Jenna, and Jenna leans in closer. Her bag shifts and I see something glint on the strap. Something I swear I've seen before. A rose gold medallion, hanging on a rose gold chain. Flat and shiny, with letters engraved in cursive on the front.

JCM.

My throat goes dry, my brain searching for where and when I've seen this before when Mimi comes out of the back. She winks at me, but then her eyes snag on something. They go wide, and before I know it, she's coming around the giant glass pastry case and heading straight for Jenna and her mom.

"Nora?" Mimi says. "Is that you?"

Jenna's mom startles but then relaxes when she sees Mimi. It's hard not to smile when you see Mimi—she's all full hips and rosy cheeks and wild curly hair, the epitome of comfort. Still, Jenna's mom says my mom's name, and my mouth turns into a desert.

"It is you!" Mimi says, wrapping up the woman in her arms. "When did you guys move back?"

"Last week," Jenna's mom says. Nora. Nora . . . I hunt through my memory for the name, but I can't find it. Still, as Mimi squeezes her tight, there's something familiar about her dark brown hair and thick bangs, her sharp nose. Jenna stands there with her head down, shifting her weight, making that medallion sway. She catches my eye. I open my mouth to say something, anything, but she looks away super fast.

"What is happening?" Marnie asks.

"I don't know," I say, but deep down, pieces are coming together. They're fuzzy and slow, but as I look at Jenna, at her mom, at that engraved medallion, I—

"And is this Jennifer?" Mimi says, releasing Nora and

smiling at Jenna. "My goodness, you look so different. So grown up."

Jennifer.

Jenna smiles and plays with the ends of her hair. "Hi, Ms. Lorenson-Woods."

JCM.

"I love your red hair," Mimi says. "So sophisticated."

Jennifer Catherine McCaffrey.

"Oh, don't get her started," Nora says. "Last month it was bright blue. I'm sure that bathroom still smells like bleach."

Jenna just smiles again and looks down at the floor. As for me, my mouth is hanging so wide open, my jaw is starting to hurt. My stomach wriggles like it's morphed into a fish out of water flopping on the dry sand, and I'm pretty sure my lungs are closing. Fast and sure. Yep, absolutely can't breathe.

"Syl?" Marnie says. "What is it?"

But I can't answer. I'm eight years old again, soggy tights, the prettiest girl in second grade laughing at me with mean brown eyes. Jennifer. Jenna.

"What brings you back to Landry Falls?" Mimi asks.

Nora and Jenna glance at each other, something sad floating between them. "Just . . . it was time to come home," Nora says.

Mimi nods, her smile smaller, sympathetic. "And just in time for Falls Fest tomorrow."

Nora nods. "Yes, we've missed that. Seattle was nice, but wasn't nearly as homey and comforting as Landry Falls in October."

"Well, welcome home," Mimi says. "If there's anything Kristin and I can do to help you settle in, let us know, okay?"

Nora nods, squeezing Jenna closer. I hold my breath, waiting for Mimi to walk away, because she knows all about Jennifer and what she did to me back in elementary school, so surely Mimi wouldn't want to prolong this reunion any longer than necessary, but then she opens her too-social, too-hospitable mouth again.

"Sylvie, sweetie?" she calls to me.

I swallow.

"Look who's back, honey."

I stare.

"Um, Syl?" Marnie whispers. "You know her?"

"No," I say.

"Well, your mom sure knows her."

I huff out a breath, my throat already tightening. I never told Marnie about Soggy Sylvie. There was never any reason to. By the time she came into my life, that was all over, Jennifer was gone, and I didn't feel like rehashing why I used to be the loneliest girl on the planet. Especially not with a potential new friend I wanted to impress. I knew Marnie would be sympathetic and defiant and would probably want to kick Jennifer's butt, but I still kept that secret close. Now I feel like it's about to spill everywhere, seeping out of my eyes and ears and fingertips.

"Jennifer, would you like to join Sylvie and her friend Marnie for some homework?" Mimi asks.

She hates me. My own mother hates me.

"I'll bring over some hot chocolate and scones, on the house," Mimi says.

I try to communicate with her telepathically, thinking really hard the words *no* and *stop* and *are you delusional* but she's not getting it.

"That would be really nice," Nora says, nudging Jenna with her shoulder. Then she looks over at me. "Hi, Sylvie, how are you?"

I nod. I think I nod. Marnie kicks me.

"Fine!" I say, except I end up yelling it.

"So what do you say?" Mimi asks, looking between Jenna and her mom.

"Oh . . . I don't know," Jenna says.

I hold my breath.

"Come on over," Marnie says, waving at Jenna.

Now it's my turn to kick her, which I do, very hard.

"Ow!" she yelps, then leans forward and whispers, "Isn't this what you wanted?"

But I don't have a chance to answer, because Nora is guiding a very pale-looking Jenna to our table. She deposits her into the chair on the other side of me and kisses the top of her head.

"I'll be back for you in an hour," Nora says, and then she's off, complimentary coffee in her hand, while Mimi announces that salted-caramel scones are forthcoming. She gives me *a look* before disappearing into the back.

I sit stiff as a board. My breathing is loud through my nostrils, like I'm a bull about to charge.

"Hey, I'm Marnie," my traitorous best friend says.

"Jenna," my nemesis says.

"Jennifer," I correct.

Both of their heads swivel toward me.

"What?" Marnie says.

"It's Jennifer," I say, and my nemesis stares at me. Even though my stomach is in knots, I stare right back. "Right?"

"I . . . I go by Jenna now," Jenna-Jennifer-Whoever says. "Since about two years ago."

"Okay . . . ," Marnie says, looking between Jenna and me. "How do you two know each other?"

"We don't," I say. Jenna says nothing. I look down at my homework. My chest feels tight; my heart is a wild horse trapped behind my ribs. Tears—actual tears—threaten to spill from my eyes. I've got to get out of here.

Now.

"Sylvie," Jenna says as I try to suck air into my constricted lungs while simultaneously pretending that I'm not at all trying to suck air into my constricted lungs.

I glance at her, my nostrils flaring. She stares back, dark eyes behind glasses, which she definitely didn't have in elementary school. Now that I look at her closely, despite the new specs and red hair and way-taller frame, I do see the old Jennifer. I don't know how I missed it before. I guess my brain was too busy sending the *Cute Girl! Cute Girl!* alert through my whole body.

Because, dang it, she is really cute.

"I'm . . . listen, I . . ." She huffs out a breath. Swallows. Picks at her fingernails, which are painted a seafoam green. "I'm sorry."

My brows dip so low I feel them brush my lashes. "You're sorry."

She looks down, takes another deep breath.

"For . . . ?" Marnie asks, but I ignore her. I know she'll grill me later anyway. Deep down, I realize this shouldn't be a big deal. It was years ago. Six, to be exact. Over two since Jenna moved away. But right now, I'm Soggy Sylvie again and all my attempts at deep breathing are failing. Majorly. Blood rushes through my ears, heartbeats are everywhere. Oh God, my eyes are wet. I'm for real about to cry. Cannot. Can. Not.

"Scones!" Mimi says, appearing at our table with a pastry-laden plate, rosy cheeks, and a cheery tone that would put Cinderella's fairy godmother to shame. She sets the plate down just as I push out my chair.

"I've gotta go," I say, grabbing my books and shoving them into my bag.

"Sylvie, honey—" Mimi starts, but I'm already gone, flying out the door and all but running down the leaf-strewn sidewalk toward our house three blocks away.

FALLS FEST IS LEGENDARY IN LANDRY FALLS. Held the second weekend of October at Braselton's Farm, it's our town's version of a fall festival, complete with pumpkin patches, hayrides, spiced cider, candy apples and funnel cakes, a corn maze, and, of course, Sugar & Star's pumpkin bread, scones, and muffins.

Marnie meets me by our bakery's tent at sundown. After I help Mom and Mimi set up a mountain of pastries, my moms send me off with a kiss and a twenty-dollar bill in my pocket for a night of revelry. They never make me work on Falls Fest, instead letting me run wild as long as I stay at the fest and, you know, observe Stranger Danger and all that.

"Where to first?" I ask Marnie. I haven't seen her

since yesterday, when I skipped out on her and Jenna at the bakery. I don't know how long she sat there with my mortal enemy and I don't want to know.

Except Marnie, apparently, is going to tell me.

"I told Jenna we'd meet her by the corn maze" falls right out of her mouth like she's talking about the color of spring leaves.

I freeze, slowly inhale the buttery fried-food scents all around us. "You did what now?"

Marnie loops one arm through mine and pulls, forcing me to stumble along next to her. "She's nice, Syl."

"So is sugar, but it'll kill you in the end."

"Drama much?"

"Betray your best friend much?"

She tips her head back and laughs. "Oh, right. Me trying to hook you up with the girl of your dreams. I'm a regular Brutus."

The corn maze looms closer and closer and my stomach flips like the Looping Starship. "She's not the girl of my dreams."

Marnie eyes me over her shoulder. "Yesterday, you were ready to propose to her."

"I was not!" Blood spills into my cheeks, my gut, my fingertips.

"What's going on, Syl? I know you know her and she knows you."

"Did . . . did she say anything?"

"No. I didn't ask. After you left, I just sort of changed the subject, talked about school and stuff."

I breathe out, knowing I've got to come clean. Marnie squeezes my arm tighter, holding on to me while I get up the nerve. Then I tell her everything, the whole soggy story and how it made me feel, the years of friendless existence until middle school.

When I'm finished, she wraps her other arm around me and hugs me tight. "That sounds awful."

"It wasn't great."

She lets me go, peering intently into my eyes.

"What?" I ask.

"Nothing," she says softly, biting her lip. "It's just, you were eight. She was eight. Everyone is hideous at eight, and it seems like she feels bad."

"Good."

"Syl. Just give her a chance."

"Why should I?"

"Because . . . people deserve second chances, especially for stupid stuff they did as little kids." Marnie pauses and waves at someone up ahead. Someone with cute red hair and cute glasses and cute freckles and cute black jeans and cute—

I squeeze my eyes shut. If I don't look, I can't see all the cuteness.

"If she ends up being heinous, we'll never talk to her again, okay?" Marnie says.

"Promise?" I say, keeping my eyes closed.

"You're such a dork. But, yes, if she's a jerk to you, she's on the no-friend list forever and ever."

I relax and barely have time to nod my consent before Marnie grabs my hand and pulls me along the grass. I smell hay and dirt. Someone bumps into me, tells me to watch where I'm going. But I just keep tripping along in my blissful darkness until Marnie pulls me to a stop.

Which is exactly when I realize the flaw in my plan and that I'm now standing right in front of Jenna with my eyes closed like the complete and utter dork that I am.

"Um . . . hey?" I hear her say.

Cute voice, my romance-addled heart says.

Shut up, my practical, self-preserving brain says.

"Hey, Jenna," Marnie says, then she squeezes my hand hard enough to hurt. "Say hello, Sylvie."

I open my eyes and God, she's even cuter up close. Hundreds of fairy lights, all strung from tent to tent throughout the festival grounds, shed a golden glow over everything. They glisten through her hair, sparkle in her eyes.

I swallow.

"Thanks . . . thanks for meeting me," she says.

"No problem," Marnie says back, even though Jenna is looking at me. Even though I'm looking at Jenna.

"Okay, so . . . ," Marnie says, then juts her thumb toward the maze's entrance. "Shall we go all *Children of the Corn?*"

"Sure," Jenna says.

"Actually, I think I'll—"

But Marnie yanks me inside the maze before I have a chance to run. I toss her a dirty look, and she makes a kissy face at me.

We follow the maze, walls of corn rising up on either side to create dozens of little passageways. Throughout the journey, I keep stealing glances at Jenna. Every time I do, I find that she's stealing glances at me too. Our eyes keep bumping into each other's. Once, she even smiles at me, and dang it, my mouth tips up at the corners in response. She's quiet, which I don't remember from elementary school. She was a chatterbox back then; teachers could hardly get her to shut up. This is an altogether different girl, something almost sad and distant behind her eyes.

By the time we spill out of the exit, straw stuck to our shirts and hair, I'm exhausted and more than a little confused.

"Ferris wheel next!" Marnie says, grabbing both of our hands and pulling us toward the huge rotating ride.

"Marnie, wait—" I say, ready to suggest a funnel cake break or something where I can easily bolt into the crowd.

My BFF is not having it, though. She guides us into the line for the Ferris wheel, pushing Jenna and me together as she drops our hands. My fingers brush Jenna's and I snap my arm back like I've been electrocuted. Jenna's gaze skitters away from mine, her teeth closing over her lower lip.

"Chill out," I whisper-hiss to Marnie, who's now standing behind us and looking as innocent as a newborn, all wide eyes and gentle smile.

I roll my eyes and turn from her as the line gathers behind us, hemming us in on all sides. The Ferris wheel rises up above us, a giant circle of soft lights and swinging buckets. When we reach the front and hand over our tickets, I turn to Marnie so she can get in the bucket first, which can easily hold all three of us.

Except Marnie's staring down at her phone. "Oh, shoot." She snaps her fingers.

"What?" I ask.

"My dads want a family picture by the merry-go-round."

"What," I say again, not a question this time. More like a dagger-eyed threat. I know for a fact that Marnie's dads want no such thing because Tim is in San Francisco on a business trip.

"Next!" the dude manning the ride bellows. His name tag reads Stan.

"Bummer," Marnie says, edging toward an opening in the line between a guy with bright blue hair and a group of girls all dressed in identical black tulle skirts.

"Marnie," I say, reaching for her. "Do not."

"Sorry, Syl, I'll text you later, okay?" She winks at me, shoots me a thumbs-up. "Bye, Jenna!"

Jenna waves as Marnie disappears into the crowd.

"On or off?" Stan yells.

"Oh," I say. "Um—"

"Come on, move it!" someone a few people back in line shouts.

"Sylvie, go!" someone else yells.

I squeeze my eyes shut, my chest suddenly tight and scratchy.

But then a hand slips into mine, palm to palm.

"Come on," a cute voice says.

Jenna. I'm so shocked by the physical contact, the way her hand feels like it fits perfectly in mine, I don't even fight it as she leads me into the bucket and Stan drops the metal bar over us.

When the ride jolts into motion, she lets go of my hand. "Wow, that was subtle."

I manage to look at her as the ground gets farther and farther away. "You mean Marnie?"

She nods.

I sigh and rub my forehead. "I feel weirdly manipulated."

She laughs a little. "Ferris wheel ride? A bucket for two? Feels like something right out of a romance novel."

I freeze.

She freezes too as what she just said settles between us.

"R-r-romance novel?" I stammer.

Her knuckles whiten on the bar across our laps. "I mean . . . um . . . you know . . ."

But no, no, I don't know. Or maybe I *do* know and it's completely freaking me out. My mind whirls, trying to think of any other reason Jenna would compare *her* and *me* sitting in a Ferris wheel to a *romance* novel.

My mind comes up with zilch.

I risk a glance. Her cheeks are splotchy and pink, and she's staring straight ahead like she's bracing for a zombie to take a bite out of her.

"Are . . . are you . . . ?" I start, but have no clue how to finish that sentence.

She swallows, but then turns to look at me. Tilts her head. "Are . . . are you?"

I blow out a breath as the Ferris wheel continues to rotate, inching us closer to the amazing view at the very top. If you'd asked me a week ago if I ever dreamed I'd be coming out to Jennifer McCaffrey while spinning above Landry Falls, I would've spit in your eye.

But it's really happening and I don't know what to say or *how* to say it. I've come out already, sure, and I've had to come out a few times for people who missed it the first go-round. But this situation—me sitting next to Jennifer McCaffrey, who, despite the fact that she might be evil incarnate, is still the cutest girl I've ever seen in real life— doesn't feel like a normal coming-out.

It feels like teetering on the edge of a waterfall.

"I'm . . . I'm . . . well . . . ," I stutter. My face has to be candy-apple red right now—it's hot as a lit match. "I'm . . . um—"

"I'm bi," she says. Blurts, really, like water spilling out of a glass. Then she flushes, her face just as crimson as mine, sweat glistening on her forehead, and exhales loudly. It cost her something to say that. Like maybe she said it first so I wouldn't have to.

"At least, I think I am," she says. "I like boys, but back in sixth grade, I figured out I like girls too. And last year, I had a major crush on a nonbinary kid in my social studies class. My mom says I don't have to put a label on it yet, but . . . well . . . yeah."

I blink at her.

She blinks back. Bites her lip.

I blink some more, my heart a bucking bull in my

chest. Then I finally realize my silence is freaking her out, that by just sitting here, saying nothing, it's like sending her out to sea all alone. I know how hard it is to come out, to anyone, even when you're pretty sure they'll be cool and supportive.

And maybe she wasn't so sure about that with me. I mean, yeah, everyone knows my moms are queer, but Jennifer—*Jenna*—and I aren't exactly budding best friends over here.

"Oh," I finally say, a real zinger. Then I shake my head and get my thoughts together. "Um . . . yeah, me too. I mean, I'm not bi. At least, I don't think so. I guess you never know, but right now, I just . . . I only like girls."

She breathes out, smiles at me, nods.

Then her smile gets bigger, wider, like she couldn't stop it if she tried, her mouth revealing some very nice teeth that must've already seen a year or two of orthodontics. She looks away, laughs a little, and something really weird happens.

I smile too.

I laugh a little too.

One of those awkward, relieved, wow-that-was-almost-embarrassing-but-ended-up-being-fine kind of laughs. My stomach feels bubbly and my head swims, like I'm dizzy, which I very well might be as the Ferris wheel jolts again, depositing us at the very top.

Jennifer McCaffrey is queer.

Like me.

And she's blushing and laughing and smiling and oh my God, she's so cute.

I shake my head, trying to bring back the humiliation she put me through, the quiet, lonely years that followed. It's there, mixed in with this new feeling that I've read about a hundred times but never actually felt.

A romance novel kind of feeling.

"Wow, it's pretty up here," Jenna says. She looks out over the town, hundreds of amber lights twinkling in the distance, all of Landry Falls neighborhoods and businesses. Evergreens soar up around us, deep green in the dark, sharing their sky with us.

"Yeah" is all I can say. The word comes out shaky, whispery.

Next to me, Jenna takes a deep breath. Then another.

"Listen, Sylvie," she finally says.

I don't say anything, but I do turn to look at her. Her eyes lock with mine, hers wide and earnest. They even look a little watery.

Jennifer McCaffrey, crying?

No way.

But there she is, her lower lip trembling, eyelids blinking at light speed.

"I'm sorry," she says.

She apologized before, yesterday in Sugar & Star, but this time, the words settle around me like a blanket in the winter. A thin one—I'm still a little chilly—but it's there.

"I was a jerk back then," she goes on when I don't say anything. "I don't know why. I didn't know the name would stick like it did. I was trying to be funny, and it just . . . it wasn't."

Something loosens in my chest. Just a little. "No. It really wasn't funny at all."

"I'm so sorry."

She keeps eye contact, and it's so intense, so sincere, that I'm the one who has to look away. Suddenly it all feels so silly, nicknames from when we were *eight,* especially in light of what we just confessed to each other.

But that old ache is still there—that lonely, no-friends ache. And yeah, maybe Jenna's mean name for me wasn't totally to blame for that. I was an awkward breadstick in elementary school, unsure in my own skin, with a family that didn't quite look like everyone else's. I was trying to figure out where I fit even before Jenna dropped *Soggy Sylvie* on me.

But still. The name didn't help. It happened. It was real, and I can't forget it.

I turn to look at Jenna. She's so different now—almost fourteen, like me, about to start high school next year.

She's queer, like me. She's . . . well, she's probably a lot of things. She also looks so incredibly sad. In fact, she looked sad the day she walked into Ms. Amalfi's room, sad when she came into Sugar & Star with her mom. It's not just because of the apology she's offering—she's actually *sad*. I'm not sure what to say. Staying mad at her for a mistake she made when we were eight years old just feels like another mistake.

So I don't say it's okay. I don't nod or shrug it off. But as the Ferris wheel rocks into motion again, now taking us closer and closer to the earth, I do change the subject.

"Why did you move back to Landry Falls?"

She blinks at me, her brows dipping for a split second before she looks away. "My mom's from here. She . . . she just wanted to . . ." But then she stops and presses her lips together, but not before I see her chin wobble.

"Jenna?"

She shakes her head and wipes at a few tears before they even have the chance to fall. "Sorry."

"It's okay," I say softly. Suddenly, stupidly, my fingers tingle to hold her hand. I curl my hands into fists to keep them in place. The wheel stops again, jutting us out parallel with the ground. A crisp fall breeze stirs our hair, cools my warmed cheeks. Below us, laughter and shouts mix with festival sounds, games beeping and rides zipping through the air.

"My dad died," she finally says without looking at me. "Last spring. Leukemia."

I suck in a breath, my own yearslong ache blooming into a full, sharp sting right in the middle of my chest.

"After that," she goes on, "we tried to make our life work in Seattle, but Mom wanted to come home. So did I." She keeps gazing out at the trees, the town lights, her eyes soft and watery.

I don't know what to say. Sometimes, there isn't anything *to* say and no reason to try. I uncurl my fingers, and this time I don't fight it. I reach out and take her hand. She lets me, lacing her fingers between mine and squeezing. Then we sit like that for the rest of the ride, two queer girls—messy and mean, sad and sorry and hopeful—holding hands on top of the world.

About the Contributors

ERIC BELL is the author of *Alan Cole Is Not a Coward* and *Alan Cole Doesn't Dance,* two middle-grade novels about a gay seventh-grade boy dealing with bullies, crushes, the power of art, and coming out. The books have been nominated to the Rainbow Book List for LGBTQ Books for Children and Teens and translated into multiple languages. When not writing, Eric teaches writing classes, runs writing workshops, and edits manuscripts. He is humbled to be part of this anthology, to write alongside such wonderful authors, and to share in the mission of spreading queerness for middle-grade readers. Unlike Marcus, he does not have the power to go back in time, though if he did, he'd probably use it to make sure his pie (gluten-free or otherwise) came with just the right amount of whipped cream.

LISA JENN BIGELOW spent her childhood running wild in the Michigan woods. A graduate of Carnegie Mellon University and the University of Illinois Urbana-Champaign, she settled in the Chicago area and became a youth services librarian and writer. She is the author of several critically acclaimed novels for young people, including *Hazel's Theory of Evolution,* winner of a Lambda Literary Award, and *Drum Roll, Please.* Lisa's best friends are dogs and people who love them.

ASHLEY HERRING BLAKE (SHE/HER) is a reader, writer, and mom to two boisterous kids. She holds a master's degree in teaching and loves coffee, arranging her books by color, and cold weather. She is the author of the young adult novels *Suffer Love, How to Make a Wish,* and *Girl Made of Stars,* as well as the middle-grade novels *Ivy Aberdeen's Letter to the World, The Mighty Heart of Sunny St. James,* and *Hazel Bly and the Deep Blue Sea. Ivy Aberdeen's Letter to the World* was a Stonewall Honor Book, as well as a *Kirkus, School Library Journal,* NYPL, and NPR Best Book of the Year. Her YA novel *Girl Made of Stars* was a Lambda Literary Award finalist. You can find her on Twitter and Instagram at @ashleyhblake and on the web at ashleyherringblake.com. She lives in Georgia.

LISA BUNKER (SHE/VO/THEY) works full time as a writer. Her first novel, *Felix Yz*, is about a boy fused with an alien. Her second novel, *Zenobia July*, is about a trans girl who gets to live as a girl for the first time in a new family and school and who investigates a cyber crime. Over the years she has made homes in New Mexico, Southern California, Seattle, the Florida Panhandle, and Maine. She currently lives in Exeter, New Hampshire, with her wife, Dawn Huebner, a child psychologist and author in her own right. Between them they have three grown children. Since 2018, Lisa has served her town in the New Hampshire House of Representatives. She also constructs crossword puzzles and, in February 2021, had her first Sunday grid published in the *New York Times*. In her leisure time, she plays chess, plays the bass, and studies languages. Her author website is lisabunker.net, and you can find her on Twitter at @LisaBunker.

ALEX GINO (THEY/THEM) is the author of the middle-grade novels *Rick; You Don't Know Everything, Jilly P!;* and the Stonewall Award–winning *George*. They love glitter, ice cream, gardening, awe-ful puns, and stories that reflect the diversity and complexity of being alive. For more information, visit alexgino.com.

JUSTINA IRELAND (SHE/HER) is the author of *Dread Nation*, a *New York Times* bestseller, as well as the sequel, *Deathless Divide*. Her earlier works include the fantasy young adult novels *Vengeance Bound* and *Promise of Shadows*. Justina also writes for the Star Wars franchise, including the books *Lando's Luck*, *Spark of the Resistance*, and the upcoming *A Test of Courage*, part of the High Republic publishing initiative. She is the former co-editor in chief of *FIYAH Literary Magazine of Black Speculative Fiction*, for which she won a World Fantasy Award. She holds a BA from Armstrong Atlantic State University and an MFA from Hamline University.

SHING YIN KHOR is a Malaysian-American Ignatz Award–winning cartoonist and immersive experience designer, exploring personal memoir, new human rituals, and collaborative world-building through graphic novels and large-scale installation art. They create comics at the intersection of race, immigrant stories, queerness, and reinterpreting Americana. They are the author of the Route 66 road-trip memoir *The American Dream?*, one of NPR's favorite books of 2019, and the historical-fiction graphic novel *The Legend of Auntie Po,* about a young Chinese-American logging-camp cook in the Sierra Nevadas reimagining Paul Bunyan tales.

MARIAMA J. LOCKINGTON (SHE/HER/HERS) is a transracial adoptee, author, and educator. She has been telling stories and making her own books since the second grade, when she wore shortalls and flower leggings every day to school. Her debut middle-grade novel, *For Black Girls Like Me,* was an ALA Notable Book, a *Booklist* Editors' Choice, a Junior Library Guild Gold Standard title, and a Project LIT Book Club Selection, and has earned five starred reviews from *Shelf Awareness, Publishers Weekly, BookPage, School Library Journal,* and *Booklist.* Mariama's second middle-grade novel, *In the Key of Us,* will be out in 2022, and her debut YA novel, *Forever Is Now,* is also forthcoming. Mariama calls many places home, but currently lives in Kentucky with her wife and her little sausage dog, Henry. You can find her on Twitter at @marilock and on Instagram at @forblackgirlslikeme.

MARIEKE NIJKAMP (SHE/THEY/ANY) is a #1 *New York Times* bestselling author of novels, graphic novels, and comics, including *This Is Where It Ends, Even If We Break,* and *The Oracle Code.* Marieke's short stories can be found in several anthologies. Marieke is a storyteller, dreamer, globe-trotter, and geek.

CLARIBEL A. ORTEGA (SHE/THEY) is a former reporter who writes YA and middle-grade fantasy inspired by her Dominican heritage. When she's not busy turning her obsession with eighties pop culture, magic, and video games into books, she's streaming on her Twitch and YouTube gaming channel, *RadBunnie,* or helping authors navigate publishing with her consulting business, Gifgrrl. Claribel has been featured on BuzzFeed, *Bustle, Good Morning America,* and *Deadline.* Claribel's debut middle-grade novel, *Ghost Squad,* is out now and is being made into a feature film.

MARK OSHIRO (HE/THEY) is the award-winning author of *Anger Is a Gift* (Schneider Family Book Award) and *Each of Us a Desert.* Their middle-grade debut, *The Insiders,* is out in 2021. When not writing, they run the online Mark Does Stuff universe and are trying to pet every dog in the world.

MOLLY KNOX OSTERTAG (SHE/HER) is a cartoonist and animation writer living in Los Angeles with her wife and pets. She is the author of the middle-grade Witch Boy graphic novel series and the young adult romance *The Girl from the Sea.* Interests outside of art include camping, cooking, and other hobbit-like activities.

AIDA SALAZAR (SHE/HER/ELLA) is an arts activist, a translator, and the award-winning author of the novels *The Moon Within* (International Latino Book Award, Américas Honor Book, Golden Poppy Award), *Land of the Cranes* (NCTE Charlotte Huck Honor Book, Jane Addams Peace Honor Book, California Library Association's John and Patricia Beatty Award), and the forthcoming *A Seed in the Sun.* She is also the author of the picture books *Jovita Wore Pants: The Story of a Revolutionary Fighter* and *In the Spirit of a Dream: 13 Stories of American Immigrants of Color.* Aida is co-editor, with Yamile Saied Méndez, of the anthology *My New Gift: Stories About Menstruation by BIPOC Authors.* She is a founding member of Las Musas, a Latinx kid lit author collective. Visit her at AidaSalazar.com.

A. J. SASS (HE/THEY) is an author, editor, and competitive figure skater who is interested in how intersections of identity, neurodiversity, and allyship impact story narratives. He is the author of *Ana on the Edge* and *Ellen Outside the Lines.* He currently lives in the San Francisco Bay Area with his boyfriend, a handful of aquarium fish, and two cats who act like dogs. Visit him online at sassinsf.com or on Twitter and Instagram at @matokah.

Resources

THE TREVOR PROJECT is the leading national organization providing crisis intervention and suicide prevention services to lesbian, gay, bisexual, transgender, queer, and questioning young people under age twenty-five. The Trevor Project has a staff of trained counselors available for support 24/7. If you are in crisis, feeling suicidal, or in need of a safe and judgment-free place to talk, call the TrevorLifeline now at 1-800-488-7386 or text "START" to 678-678.

THE NATIONAL SUICIDE PREVENTION LIFELINE provides 24/7 free and confidential support for people in distress, prevention and crisis resources for you or your loved ones, and best practices for professionals. You can find out more at suicidepreventionlifeline.org. If you need help now, text "START" to 741-741 to immediately connect with help at the Jed Foundation or call 1-800-273-TALK (8255) for services with the National Suicide Prevention Lifeline.